272

mp

CW00551243

(29) (30) (32) (47) (111) (117)
27 sp
67
118 sp
109
142 sp
146 sp

cl

THE DAYS OF YOUR FATHERS

GEOFFREY HOUSEHOLD

THE DAYS
OF YOUR
FATHERS

LONDON
MICHAEL JOSEPH

First published in Great Britain by Michael Joseph Ltd
27 Wrights Lane, London W8 5TZ
1987

British Library Cataloguing in Publication Data

Household, Geoffrey
   The days of your fathers.
   I. Title
   823'.912[F]   PR6015.07885

   ISBN 0–7181–2808–7

Phototypeset in Great Britain by
Input Typesetting Ltd, London.
Printed and bound by Billing & Sons Ltd
London and Worcester.

Contents

Kangaroo Loves Me

He wore a bowler hat. There was a faded velvet collar on his dark-blue overcoat. His gaily striped tie was worn and greasy with years of constant use. His teeth were decayed. One knew at first sight that he was married to a woman much bigger than himself. He was obviously a Londoner.

He had no part in the New York crowd of the nineteen twenties. A townsman, yet racy of the soil, his place was in some pub of the London suburbs, where the landlord was a dog fancier and the local bookmaker had his sacred corner table and the best chair in the saloon bar. The odour that his memory most lovingly selected was a mixture of beer and iodine; so the pub had smelt whenever a new litter of prize terriers entered the world, and their little tails were being docked on the bar before a choice crowd of the landlord's favourites. He had often held the pup; the dirty hands were very gentle. He had been a favourite of the bookmaker, too. Knew a bit about the gees, he did. His bandy legs suggested an early training as a stableboy, and indeed he had ridden a race or two, but lost his job before he was old enough to know when and how to drink.

He stood before one of the kangaroo enclosures in the Bronx Zoo. A female kangaroo lay on her side close to the wire, listening to him. She reclined in the curious manner of kangaroos: full length and leaning on one elbow, like a Roman lady at a banquet. Her grey underside was luxuriously displayed. With her spare paw she fanned the flies from her nose. She watched him with languorous interest, and waved her ears when he spoke to her.

The crowd, a cross-section of central Europe, loud-mouthed, well fed, and feeding as they walked, passed by the kangaroos with little interest; they were bound for the

1

capybara and the ant-eater, distorted creatures to which they had a certain affinity. When people joined him at the railing, he glanced sidelong at them like a fox. If they belonged to the usual run of visitors, he ducked his peaked head into his dirty butterfly collar and waited resignedly till they moved on; but if the intruder was a man, and alone, and likely to be sympathetic, he motioned to him to be still. He showed uncanny judgement in picking those whom he chose to trust. They seldom let him down, but watched, smiling, while he continued the interrupted conversation.

'Ain't yer a lil bleeder?' he would say softly. 'Like to be back in Austrylia, wouldn't yer?'

His voice was a caress of curious vowel sounds. The kangaroo fanned herself, and listened with obvious delight.

His name was Breown – so he pronounced it, and his associates, to whom such immigrant names as Szczewc were easy because they never saw them written, took him at his own valuation of it. His wife was a roaring Irish-American, red-faced and bulging. She ran a small hand laundry of her own. He had the reputation of a good-for-nothing little Britisher, who would be on the breadline if not for her. It was true that she supported him; yet he would have willingly slaved for some colourless little woman of his own breed. Kate's overpowering vitality sapped his self-respect. A dog would have been something to live for, even to work for, but he hadn't the heart to bring up a pup in a New York tenement. He hungered for the monotonous rows of small, sordid houses on the outskirts of London, each with its own back garden where a dog could run loose and there was room for a hutch of ferrets or Belgian hares.

Kate was not unkind, but she was no object for tenderness. She was a mother to men; a brazen, foul-mouthed mother who liked them rebellious and hard-fisted. Her husband was neither. She treated him with a good-humoured contempt, and was unfaithful to him on the rare occasions when she aroused a passing desire. He was surrounded by contempt – even at Mike's, where the salted, ethered beer kept up some semblance of a saloon, and he should have been in his element. But Mike's customers

2

knew little of dogs, and of horses less. Of heavy badinage they knew all there was to know, and he was their butt.

Until he discovered the Bronx Park, and the inner shrine which housed his slender and gentle kangaroo, he had no creature to appreciate the sensitiveness that was his birthright. Twice a week for more than a year he had visited her. On every occasion he risked the three-dollar fine and brought her a carrot. For nine months he threw it over the netting. Then on one triumphant day, and ever since, she had taken it from his hand. Only one carrot he gave her at each visit, for he respected the rights of the zoological society, and did not wish to interfere with her carefully balanced diet.

The kangaroo gave him an ambition. It was very long since he had had one. If you had asked him what he most wanted, he would have answered: 'To get 'ome agyne.' But that was a mere longing, like the hope of the pious to go to Heaven; the difficulties seemed so immense that he never even planned return to England. His ambition was more definite. It might be attained. It was a desire that sweetened the hour in bed before he slept, and took away the bitterness of waking.

One day he overcame his fear of ridicule, and demanded boldly that his desire be granted. He swallowed before speaking, and his scraggy Adam's apple bobbed up and down.

'Lemme in the kyge with 'er,' he begged the keeper.

'Against the rules,' answered the keeper shortly – he was not a little jealous of Mr Breown's conquest. 'And don't you kid yourself that you've made friends with her. Those kangaroos are the timidest animals in the gardens.'

'Cripes! Timidest animals in the gordens! Yer don't say!' he muttered, deeply impressed.

He slunk away, hurt and disappointed, but his pride in his achievement increased. He did not know he was proud. It took the form of increased pity for the kangaroo.

'She ain't got no call to be timid,' he murmured indignantly. ''Oo's going to 'urt 'er? That's what I'd like ter know! 'Oo's going to 'urt 'er?'

3

He understood that he would never persuade the keeper to let him into the cage. The result of his disappointment was an orgy of poisonous whisky that left him whiter and spottier than ever. But the orgy was not bad for him spiritually. It was followed by an intense need to assert himself, which led him to use his brain. His cockney cunning, long unemployed for want of any worthy cause, came back to him.

The municipal elections were not far off. He sat in Mike's, drinking cautiously, and dribbling a nasty stream of cockney irony against the Democrats. His tongue was a keen weapon, but he had ceased to use it on personalities, for the sallies which would have set a London pub rocking with laughter were lost in Mike's. His comments on the public administration found listeners; the style passed unheeded, but the eloquence alone won attention. The district leader, white slip under his waistcoat, gold watch-chain across his ample stomach, was forced to take notice of this attack. He asked Mr Breown what the Democrats could do for him. Mr Breown told him.

'Aw, come on now! Talk plainly, can't you?'

'I tell yer that's what I want,' repeated the little man. 'Get me into the kangaroo kyge, and I'll shut me 'ead!'

Enough of his race remained in the Jew to enable him to recognise a spiritual need when he saw one. He agreed to do his best.

It wasn't easy; but the district leader, his interest stirred both by the oddness of Mr Breown's ambition and by the difficulty of realising it, went far up in the hierarchy of Tammany Hall to get permission. Eventually he got it.

The Londoner dressed as if for his wedding. He was conscious of the same feeling of excitement. It was purer excitement, for he had been afraid of Kate. His marriage to her was a desperate effort to make the new country liveable – as if by changing his manner of life he could change his tastes. He had no fear at all of this second wedding. He would have liked to buy himself a new suit for the occasion. But the kangaroo knew the smell of his old

4

suit. She might be nervous of a new smell. Better not risk it.

In the subway he was very still and tense. He hated the subway – chiefly because it wasn't the London tube – and took a perverse pleasure in losing himself on it that he might add fuel to his grievance. He did not lose himself on this journey, though Mott Avenue offered him the only genuine chance in New York to do so.

He had stipulated that the interview was to take place after the public had left the gardens. He slipped through the gates a quarter of an hour before closing time. He walked unseeing past the yaks and the ostriches, but stopped to say a word to the emu. The bird came from Australia, the same country as his beloved.

Waiting for him by the kangaroo paddocks were the district leader, his little boy, and two friends. The district leader had a healthy human curiosity, sometimes offensive in its outward manifestations, but always kindly. Nevertheless, Mr Breown resented his presence. It seemed an intrusion on his privacy that made him flush with unreasoning anger. He comforted himself deliberately with the thought that for once he was the centre of interest.

'Timidest animal in the gordens! Er-r, I'll show 'em!'

But even the fame which he knew he would win did not compensate him. It was like making capital out of the timidity of a bride.

His audience greeted him with the gibes of crude good-fellowship, slapping him on the back, telling him he'd forgotten his whip and uniform, begging him to put his head in the kangaroo's mouth. He stepped jauntily to the cage, acting, acting, with an absurd feeling of disloyalty to his kangaroo.

''Ere y'are, gen'l'men! Walk up and see Mr 'Arry Breown do 'is fymous act!'

The keeper unlocked the door.

'She won't let you touch her,' he growled disgustedly. 'I never saw a kangaroo yet that would let itself be handled.'

The little cockney entered the cage, and crept softly through the door in the partition that led to the paddock.

The kangaroo shied away from him and sat on her hind legs, startled and ready for flight. She recognised him, but he was in the wrong place. It took her some time to reconcile the contradictory fact that a friend whose essence was outside-the-cage-ness was now inside it. He sat on the step and talked to her. After ten minutes of false starts, she hopped across the paddock and rested on her tail, looking at him. He stood up very slowly and made a step towards her. She trembled and her ears moved anxiously, but she didn't stir. He talked to her until it was safe to take one more step. Once she was under the spell of his voice, he offered her the carrot. She hopped forward on hands and haunches with the ungainly motion of a kangaroo at ease and took it. While she was eating he talked to her, humourously and gently.

She lifted her head and waited for more carrot. Instead, the offering hand came nearer and touched her muzzle. She shied, but it wasn't a determined shy. She tempted him again, ears pricked like the gracious ears of an antelope. He stroked her throat and scratched her behind the ears. She lay down on one elbow. Never hurrying, always talking, he stroked the brown back and the soft grey belly. The kangaroo fanned herself with coy detachment. At last she hopped away from him.

He left the paddock, happy as he had not been happy since childhood. He simply didn't see the men who surrounded him. The keeper was generous and enthusiastic. The others, taking their cue from him, showed no less astonishment.

'She sure loves you!' exclaimed the keeper.

'Loves me?' repeated the little man, still dazed by his good fortune. 'Loves me?'

The district leader guffawed.

'And, oh boy! Is you in love with her!'

The gibe, innocently enough meant, crashed into the smooth and shining pool of his mind. He blushed, ducking his head within the butterfly collar, and walked rapidly and guiltily away.

He never went back to Kate or to the district. That was

well for him. Yet, had he done so, he would have met with a new respect. They didn't believe that he was really in love with his kangaroo.

A Jew and an Irishman

The liner plunged down the first of the great Biscay seas and met the second with a crash and shudder that set in motion all movable objects within her. The sigh of human beings, each in his prison of panelled teak or painted iron, sounded through the *Alhaurin* like a passing ghost, while a loose water-pipe, a chair sliding across the lounge, a falling shaving-brush and the crated locomotive at the bottom of No. 3 Hold mingled their sounds with a thousand others into one distant and all-pervasive groan.

Mr Flynn, finding his feet suddenly higher than his head, was inspired to raise them still higher and to kick a tattoo against the springs of the empty bunk above him.

'Danno me boy', he said loudly, 'ye've been shipped to Buenos Aires like an old maid's dream. Ye're dishonoured for ever, Danno, and the little yellow man that bought your soul will be driving you to market seven days a week. Or would they be eating horse-flesh, now, in Brazil? God help you, you have the drink taken, and there's none to listen to you!'

Danno Flynn heaved himself down his bunk until the small of his back was resting upon the foot of it. From this position he could reach the bell with his big toe; he rang it; propped up his heel on the rosette, crossed his legs and fell asleep again.

His precarious balance was disturbed by the opening of the stateroom door. Mr Flynn raised his knees to his chest, and a simultaneous and violent pitch of the ship rolled him head over heels so that he came to rest on all fours.

The steward seeing this tousled quadruped staring at him from the bunk, hesitated in surprise.

8

'Wuff!' barked Mr Flynn, joyously appreciating his own fantastic appearance. 'Wuff, wuff!'

With his dark skin, his hair falling over his eyes, and the black and grey of his unshaven bristles and untidy moustache, he looked remarkably like an irate sheep-dog.

'Is there anything you want, sir?' stammered the steward, carefully keeping all but his head and one shoulder behind the door.

'There is,' said Flynn. 'Will ye tell the Canine Defence League of Connemara that I am shipped to Buenos Aires?'

'It says on your card that you're going to Santos, sir.'

'Do you have the time now, steward?' asked Danno Flynn, seeing that conversation with this literal-minded Englishman would be difficult.

'Eight o'clock – and the second day out from London, sir.' answered the steward pointedly.

'And where the devil are we?'

'In the Bay.'

'By God, if it's a bay,' said Danno, 'the waves do be coming to dance in it from all the oceans.'

'It's the Bay of Biscay, sir,' said the steward.

'Then I'll be having a beer.'

'Sorry, sir, bar's shut.'

'Ah, to hell with you!' said Danno, rolling backwards and pulling the sheets over his head.

At mid-day the *Alhaurin* was a dripping nucleus of solidity between the low grey sky above her and the grey seas that she rode. The squalls blew up from the west, driving hard and low into the promenade decks. The spray and rain swept the main deck so that the hatches between the first and third class were low islands in a miniature surf that broke against them with every roll of the ship. There was no one about save an occasional oil-skinned seaman or officer paddling grimly to duty. Under the lee of the smoking-room two hardy Englishwomen were bundled up in chairs and regarding the Bay with well-bred contempt; they gave an impression of holding under their rugs Britannia's shield and trident.

Mr Flynn lurched out of the smoking-room, attired in an

old sweater and tweed trousers. He had neither shaved nor brushed his hair, and was wet, dirty and unsteady as the *Alhaurin* herself. He greeted the ladies loudly.

'Good morning to you!'

'A nice, fresh morning,' answered the elder Britannia cheerfully.

'It is, ma'am. But it's a poor ship, God help us!'

'Oh dear!' said the younger. 'Don't you think she's safe?'

'Safe, is it? She'd float with the gas that's in the bottled beer –' Danno raised his hand to his mouth and produced a sound as sudden and alarming as a sergeant-major's word of command '– and I ask you, ma'am, would ye have shipped to Buenos Aires and you knowing there's not a barrel of beer on her?'

'My dear,' whispered the younger Britannia, 'I'm afraid he's a little – er –'

'*Good* morning,' said the elder Britannia severely.

Danno Flynn took a turn round the promenade deck and looked in through the windows of the lounge and writing-room. The *Alhaurin* was carrying two hundred first-class passengers to the Atlantic ports of South America, most of them enjoying a three weeks' passage paid by an employer and without a worry except how to get the bar bill on to the expense account. But, under the circumstances, they were in no mood for conversation and glanced coldly at Danno's dark, dripping and cheerful face. He gripped the rails of the companion in both hands and slid from B deck to C deck, from C deck to D deck, and from D deck into a puddle of water on the main deck. In the hope of human society he splashed across to the immigrant saloon.

The *Alhaurin* in that spring of 1939 was doing good business on the outward voyage. In the third-class was a happy group of Czech and Polish peasants, contracted to work and – though they naturally did not know it – to die in the Chaco, whose passages had also been paid, and an unhappy group of thirty Central European Jews who had paid their own. The saloon stank of oilcloth, stale cucumbers and sweat. Wooden benches ran along the walls, and opposite

them were iron tables and uncompromising wooden chairs
screwed severely into the floor.

On four benches Danno saw prostrate bodies ending in
heavy knee-high boots. On another was a shapeless mound
of greasy shawls that finally resolved itself into a Polish
woman, her small son and a bundle of pitiable possessions
that she did not dare leave in the cabin. In the recess on
one side of the steward's pantry was a grave Jew in frock-
coat and skull-cap staring at nothing and moving his lips,
and in the other recess was a tall girl in a blue sweater and
skirt with a red ribbon round her dark head. She was
reading, and had bare, slim, impatient and rather furry legs
which ended in sandals.

'Good morning to you,' said Danno to the barman.

'Good morning, sir.'

'Have you a beer, steward?'

'Draught or bottled, sir?'

'Now would ye believe that I must walk through six inches
of raging ocean to quench my thirst when they have but to
carry a barrel up a pair of ladders?' asked Danno
triumphantly. 'I'll have draught, me boy, and will you take
one with me?'

'Thank you, sir.'

'And the lady, too. Will ye have a beer, ma'am, or a drop
of what you fancy?'

'Thank you,' said the girl with a slight foreign accent, 'but
I don't drink.'

'Ah, and what would ye say to that?' exclaimed Danno,
unabashed.

He turned to the old man on the other side.

'Will your reverence take a beer?' he asked.

The Jew looked up, startled, and met Mr Flynn's dancing
eyes. What had been said to him he did not know, but,
seeing that he had to deal with a rowdy, aggressive, powerful
and incomprehensible Gentile, he assumed that it had been
an insolence. He did not reply, and returned with dignity
to his meditation.

'By God, 'tis an unsociable ship!' said Danno Flynn.

'He didn't understand you,' explained the girl. 'My father speaks hardly any English.'

'Like me grandad,' Danno replied. 'But he'd understand if you asked him what he'd take – for it was not often he heard them words, he being the thirstiest man in Connemara. Beer?' he asked very loudly. 'Will ye take a beer?'

He swayed to the motion of the ship, the surface of the beer in his glass forming an acute angle to the level of the floor. The girl's father, overcome by this phenomenon and the effort of concentrating his thoughts on a wet and noisy barbarian, collapsed upon the table with a groan.

Danno slid a hand under his shoulders and deposited him at full length on the bench with a rug under his head. His movements were so swift and confident that, though the girl had rushed simultaneously to her father, there was nothing for her to do but flutter anxiously around him.

'What is it?' she sobbed. 'He is worn out. Is there a doctor? Get me a doctor!'

'I am a doctor meself,' said Danno, 'so let you not be troubling your pretty head. 'Tis the sea-sickness, and that's all. I should not have been disturbing his reverence the way he is, making meself the last straw that turns the camel's stomach.'

'Will it pass? Are you sure it will pass?'

'He'll be easy when 'tis calm,' answered Danno positively. 'Is it the first time he is at sea?'

'The first time that either of us are at sea,' she replied.

'Ah, to be sure! You'll come from a far country.'

'From Austria.'

'And have you famine there? Or would there be war with the English?'

'Dear God! Don't you read newspapers?' she asked.

'Every Saturday,' said Danno unashamed. 'But would I be troubling meself with all them queer people? But I remember now. Austria – 'tis where the Nazis murdered the little president and would not let him see a priest, and dancing in the streets they were, and holding up their hands to show the blood on them. Sure, it is no place for a woman.'

12

'It is,' she answered indignantly. 'Vienna is a lovely town for any woman.'

'Then why did ye leave it?'

'I am a Jewess,' she replied, trying to keep a neutral tone to her voice, and furious with herself for caring what tone of voice she used, for finding it necessary to avoid either fear or challenge or pride. To say 'I am a Jewess' brought into play a hundred complex humiliations, of which the strongest was resentment that there should be anything at all in so simple a statement worthy of such violent emotions.

'Well, and aren't they saying the Irish are the thirteenth tribe?' asked Danno Flynn cordially. 'Or is it the twelfth? God help me, I am always miscounting the tribes and the holy apostles. All I know, 'tis the thirteenth is unlucky.'

The smell of the saloon and the strain of listening to a foreign dialect were too much for her.

'Oh, please!' she cried. 'You will excuse me. I – I am tired!'

She rushed into the open air. The wind picked up her slim, swaying body and carried it away.

'To be sure, 'tis not all of us have voyaged to Liverpool with the cattle as I have meself,' remarked Danno. 'Will ye have a beer, steward?'

The *Alhaurin* slid sideways down an invisible slope and recovered her balance with a lurch like that of a self-conscious drunk. A crate of bottles glided across the floor of the pantry, and the steward grabbed the edge of his sink with both hands. Danno Flynn, seeing the back of his neck turn from brown to green, gave up hope of further conversation and returned to his cabin in the first-class.

Mr Flynn spent the following day drinking beer in the third-class saloon from eleven to one, and six to eleven. While the ship was in Lisbon and the bar closed, he slept it off; but when the steward, half-way down the Tagus, opened his hatch, he let in the upper half of Mr Flynn's waiting body and began to serve his charges with Mr Flynn's free drinks.

The peasant immigrants did not worry themselves to account for the continual visitor. If, having a first-class ticket, he chose to drink in the third-class bar, they assumed – those of them who were intelligent enough to assume anything – that it was because the drinks were cheaper. To the Jews, however, he was a mystery. They could not understand why anyone should prefer the cheerless, reeking immigrant saloon to the luxury, envied and therefore exaggerated, of the first-class; but most of them, sitting in melancholy resignation before the punishment their God had inflicted on them, welcomed Mr Flynn as a comparatively pleasant chastisement. His only demand was that somebody should drink his beer and attempt to understand his conversation.

The Austrian girl, Berta Feitel, was thoroughly puzzled by him. She was fascinated by his shimmer of charm, drunk or sober – it was too light-hearted a quality to be common among her own people or indeed among any city-dwellers – but his wild exuberance seemed to her unreal, a part acted for some purpose of his own. She longed for her father to come on deck. Having spent a wise and simple life between the schools and the synagogue, he had a peculiar gift of seeing to the heart of any human being, and he could have summed up Danno Flynn for her. But Mr Feitel was still in his bunk, continually sick though the sea was calm, and Berta had no wisdom to fall back on but the experience of her own agitated youth.

When Mr Flynn was not present, he was the chief topic in the third-class quarters. Berta was supposed to be the authority on him, since she spoke good English and had always mixed freely with Gentiles. She could not always avoid being cross-examined.

'Oy, Berta! What has he been telling you? A doctor? That man? Of course he is no doctor! Did he tell you so, Berta?'

Her questioner laughed irritatingly, making a sound like *fee-fee-fee* through his little round mouth. He had a gross body, a pink and featureless face, and the habit of generally being right. She disliked him intensely – the more so, since it occurred to her that there was an air about doctors, Jewish or Gentile, that Mr Flynn certainly did not possess.

14

'Why should he not be?' asked a small dark chess-player, coming to the rescue. 'He is an intellectual. I do not understand all he says, but he is an intellectual!'

'That was what you said of the grocer on the corner,' answered the fat man mercilessly. 'And he kicked you, Jacob, scrubbing the pavement.'

The chess-player sighed at this memory, and returned to his problem.

'At any rate he has no prejudice,' said Berta.

'Ach, that is because you are a pretty girl!' lisped the practical man. 'He means you to trust him. He listens and overhears what we say. He makes us drunk. Jacob, he is paid to be here!'

The chess-player looked up, startled and serious.

'It is true,' he said. 'I will be careful. I will be careful.'

The Jewish corner of the saloon became full of quick, restless movement. Some put their hands in their pockets to feel if letters were still there; some sighed, imperceptibly rocking their bodies; others glanced at the door. Doors were no longer innocent bits of wood for them. Bad news came through doors. Berta herself was affected. Not even on the high seas was one safe. Everywhere, everywhere there were spies.

Five days of irrigation with beer quenched the drought in Danno Flynn's interior. He continued to spend some hours a day in the third-class saloon and his hospitality was as promiscuous as ever; but he drank in half-pints instead of pints, his face was shaven, his moustache neatly clipped, and his body sportingly dressed.

When one evening he turned up in a boiled shirt and dinner jacket, a hush descended upon the saloon. The peasants shuffled their preposterous boots, stared and breathed very loudly. Such raiment was connected in their minds with the President of the Republic, or a marriage, or the excitement of a travelling salesman; they expected Mr Flynn to unfurl a banner and pull a diamond ring or a bottle of medicine out of his pocket. Israel in exodus felt all its suspicions confirmed. He was rich. He had no good right to be there.

The silence impressed even Danno. He was, for about the third time in his life, self-conscious. He had dressed himself up for a gala dinner in the first-class and saw no reason for changing merely because he craved a draught beer. He met Berta's ironical eyes, and flushed. It occurred to him that he had been guilty of wanting to be admired, that he could, after all, have drunk whisky in his own smoking-room.

'But why wouldn't I show meself to the darling,' argued Danno loudly to himself, 'seeing she could know me for a hundred years and never see me in the like of these clothes again?'

He drank a beer with the steward and departed hastily, wishing the saloon a noisy good-night.

Meanwhile Berta had silently vanished into the night. She was filled with cold anger at his impudence in appearing amongst them with this bold admission that he belonged to another world; that he was not of them but had power over them. At the same time she knew that she herself was the cause; even the most rabid Nazi put on his best uniform when he had to deal with Jewish girls. It was the moment to ask questions, when she was at her coldest and he off his guard.

Danno emerged from the severe cubical deck-house which contained the immigrants' public rooms. The iron plates of the main deck and the tarpaulin-covered hatches were flooded with moonlight. The *Alhaurin*, at this level a ship rather than a floating hotel, swished through the calm water while a band faintly sounded from somewhere in the towering terraces of the first-class and a light flashed on the horizon, reminding the traveller that even in the wastes of the Atlantic were the Azores.

Berta leaned over the rail, waiting for her prey and comparing herself to Judith before Holofernes. As the door of the saloon slammed, she turned and smiled invitingly at Danno.

'How is your da?' he asked.

'Still sick. He cannot eat or get up.'

'I'll see him,' said Danno.

16

'It's nothing,' she answered swiftly. 'It will pass. Stay here and talk to me.'

A strand of her black hair, fragrant in spite of the saloon and the peasants and the paintwork of a stuffy cabin below the waterline, blew gently against his face.

'What land is that?' she asked, pointing to the light.

''Tis Africa,' he replied, 'with negro slaves holding up a jewel to you that you may stop and be the bride of their great king.'

'I would rather be where I am,' said Berta dreamily.

Danno felt the wind cold against his unaccustomed shirt-front as two drops of sweat shot down his chest from hair to hair like the balls on a pin-table.

'Then I would not be changing places with any king in the wide world,' he said.

He laid his hand over hers. It did not return his pressure, but remained warm and unresisting while Abraham looked down approvingly – or so Berta hoped – upon his handmaiden.

'You must know all the lands we pass so well,' she suggested, hoping to find out whether he was on regular duty with the line.

'I was always a great reader,' answered Danno cautiously, 'and many's the beating I had for it. If it was not Father Donnelly had the hide off me for not attending to my book, 'twas my Da for not attending to the sheep.'

He told her a little of his boyhood in Connemara, of the green hills and white villages, of the glimpses of the Atlantic and the soft rain that drifted inland like smoke from the sea. As he talked, it seemed to her that her suspicions had been utterly foolish. This was the history of a David rather than a Holofernes. With the readiness of youth she swung to the other extreme, telling herself that the curse of her race was to suspect, always to suspect.

'So that is why you came here, down to the third-class!' she cried with a warmth that surprised him. 'You have been poor. You like simple people – true people!'

'And what more would I need to bring me here but the sight of your face?' he answered.

17

'But you didn't know I was there. And sometimes – those first days – you did not speak to me.'

'To be sure, I did not,' he admitted penitently. 'But 'twas the sorrow of my heart at leaving Eire and the thirst that was on me that would have floated the ship from under our feet. And, God help me, it was the barrel of beer that brought me to the third-class and no other thing at all.'

'Have they no beer in the first-class?' she asked.

'Devil a drop that's fit to drink!'

It couldn't be true. Dear God, what an easy little fool he must be thinking her! All her suspicions rushed back, now the harder to bear for her moment of tenderness towards him.

'You expect me to believe that?' she cried. 'That we . . . cattle . . . down here can get something that you cannot?'

Her face was drawn and her mobile mouth twitching with anger at her own treachery. Danno Flynn stared at the explosive young woman, his features showing a sudden and comical consciousness of guilt.

'You cannot harm us!' she stormed. 'You will not be listened to, do you hear me? We are not afraid of you. Nothing can happen to us now, nothing any more. We – we snap our fingers!'

She burst into tears and ran from him. Even the beating of her feet upon the deck was angry.

''Tis the long voyage,' said Danno Flynn, 'and a young girl is a chancy thing. I should not have been telling her that I came for the beer.'

He climbed back to his own quarters and strolled into the smoking-room in the certainty of finding the ship's doctor. Part of the girl's unaccountable moodiness was due, he thought, to worry about her father. Mr Feitel ought to have been up and about long since, for the sea had been calm as a lake since they sailed from Lisbon.

Dr Pulberry was in his usual chair and was, as usual, alone. His little red face and little white moustache were perched perkily upon the high butterfly collar of his mess uniform. His brusque and hearty manner did not gain for him all the free drinks that he felt to be his due; he accepted

Mr Flynn's offer of a whisky with gratitude, made a joke about an Irishman, and, finding it well received, became very communicative.

'Yes, I've seen the old fellow,' he said in answer to Danno's questions. 'I know those cases – have 'em every voyage. Nerves! Funk! No stamina! Goes on being sick because it's less effort than exercising a little will power!'

Dr Pulberry, having retired from practice ten years since, considered that his job should be a sinecure. One patched up the crew. One discussed their ailments with the first-class passengers, especially the good-looking women. But one resented immigrants. At his age one resented them very strongly. If they didn't have infectious diseases they had diseases of malnutrition; and if they didn't have those they were seasick.

'Cannot ye give him a pill?' asked Danno.

'The usual sedatives of course! Certainly! But they don't stop him. I'll try a better cure on him soon.'

On his visit to the immigrant saloon the next morning Danno discovered that communication had become very difficult. Those passengers who had spoken English to him were absorbed in chess or meditation or excited arguments – which ceased when he drew near. Those who did speak to him, all of them fair-haired, spoke in tongues so utterly incomprehensible that Danno shouted back to them in Erse. This amusement, however, palled under the contemptuous gaze of Berta's large, clear eyes. She ignored his enquiries about her father by replying that he was better and instantly returning to her book.

Danno Flynn put a black curse upon the night that he had gone to the third-class in a dinner jacket, and passed two whole days moping in his own smoking-room and hanging over the rail for a sight of Berta as she lay peacefully on the hatch of the main deck.

Whether it was to emphasize the difference between herself and the shapeless bundles of peasant women or whether because she knew Danno would be looking, she made a habit of taking the sun for an hour a day in a yellow swimming-suit. This delightful sight led to Dr Pulberry and

19

other pillars of the bar deserting their usual chairs for chairs on the verandah.

'Now I know why you went slumming! Pretty, eh?' said the doctor, digging Danno in the ribs.

'You should not be looking at her, doctor,' said Danno severely, 'and her Da dying on you.'

'We'll have him up this very afternoon,' Dr Pulberry answered, rubbing his hands. 'Sedatives won't do it, so we'll use shock. Done it before! Always works! Come down with me about four o'clock and I'll show you.'

'Shock, is it?' asked Danno gloomily. 'If he's a decent man, 'twould be enough for him to see his daughter parading herself the way an actress would not be doing in the moving pictures, and she paid a hundred pound a week for it.'

At four o'clock Danno accompanied the doctor into the maze of passage-ways below the third-class deck. They pushed past motionless peasant women, staring blankly at nothing, and cannoned off bands of Czech and Polish children pointing fingers at each other round corners and shouting their international word – Stikummup!

Dr Pulberry hammered smartly on a cabin door and walked straight in. Mr Feitel lay in a narrow lower berth, his shoulders imprisoned between the white rail of the bunk and the cheerless, bolt-studded iron of the white bulkhead. His face was sunken and grey, and he was breathing deeply as if the tiny cabin contained all the air that he could ever reach. Berta sprang up from the opposite bunk and faced the doctor challengingly, the distrust and anxiety of her face changing, as soon as she saw Danno Flynn, to an expressionless mask in which her large eyes burned with anger.

'Captain wants you at once!' said Dr Pulberry roughly to Mr Feitel. 'Up with you!'

Berta translated to her father, who struggled painfully and raised himself on one elbow.

'What is it?' she asked. 'What have we done?'

'No business of mine,' said the doctor briskly. 'You're not

allowed to land. Wireless from the Brazilian Government –
and I expect you know why.'

Berta's voice as she poured out the Yiddish translation
to her father was like the cry of a whole people going up
to heaven against injustice.

'On deck in ten minutes!' said the doctor unmoved.
'Come on, Flynn!'

He left the cabin brusquely. Danno remained behind
watching the sick man, who sat up, swayed and fell back
again on to the pillow.

'Whatever you want to let him alone,' said Berta slowly,
as if every syllable were a tense, muscular act, 'I will give
you. Do you understand?'

'I should not be mixing myself in this,' murmured Danno
thoughtfully, feeling Mr Feitel's pulse 'but if he goes on
deck, 'twill be the death of him.'

'Leave him alone!' Berta cried. 'Don't you believe me? I
will come to you when you like.'

Danno glared at her, suddenly aware of her presence.

'And are you not ashamed to be talking so with your da
on his death-bed?' he roared. 'You will stand up now and
do what I tell you. You will go to the cook and turn your
rolling eyes on him and bring me an ounce of sugar and a
teaspoonful of baking powder.'

'What do you mean? You're no doctor!'

'I am in a manner of speaking, though 'tis sheep I treat
the most of.'

'Sheep?'

'Sure, if you saw one stand on his hind legs,' shouted
Danno, exasperated by her tone, 'you would know 'tis only
human like the rest of us. Be off with you now!'

'I will not. He shall be on deck if I carry him on my back,'
she said. 'I know your sort. You only want a chance to say
we were disobedient. Your sheep will go where you tell
them. They have learned that much!'

'The devil's in the girl!' said Danno. 'Now will ye listen?
The doctor is after telling you your Da must see the captain.
'Tis a lie – though, by Jesus, the shock would have cured

21

him if it were the sea-sickness he had! But 'tis not the sea, 'tis his stomach.'

'What do you know?' she asked contemptuously.

'Am I not telling you I am a veterinary surgeon and the best sheep-doctor in all Eire? And I know that if it were a sheep or a pig or a horse or a saint from heaven and he sea-sick, he would be breathing fast and slow and jerky as if the soul of him were in torment, and not hungry for air and breathing deep, as is your Da. 'Tis what they call acidosis he has, and though the sea started it, 'tis not the sea any longer nor the fear of the sea that turns his stomach now.'

Berta stared at him with shining eyes, from which huge tears of relief spilled on to her cheeks.

'Will ye go to the cook now,' he coaxed her, patting her hand, 'and bring me a teaspoonful of baking powder and an ounce of sugar.'

Berta nodded, and vanished down the passage. Meanwhile Danno soothed, groomed and massaged her father as if he had been a thoroughbred recovering from severe fright – which indeed he was. The old man thanked him in scraps of broken English and, when Berta returned with the remedy, took it trustfully and in absolute faith that it was going to stay down.

'Now keep him quiet, and he'll be better before night,' said Danno. 'I will tell the doctor 'twas the shock that did it, and he will be speaking of his cure from one end of the ship to the other and that pleased with himself he will order special food for your da.'

'But you'll come and see him?' asked Berta anxiously.

'You will have him on deck under the awnings tomorrow afternoon, and I will see him then. And I will send you one of them canvas chairs for him,' added Danno drily, 'so he shall not be sprawling on the hatches and the doctor and the proud English turning their opera glasses on him and jiggling their feet on the planks.'

By nightfall Mr Feitel had shown a marked improvement. A breakfast of eggs was followed by a lunch of chicken – obtained through Danno's outrageous flattery of the doctor

– and at five o'clock he was sitting in a deck-chair, watching the flying fish in the strip of blue sky and blue water between the awning and the rail, and thankful for his return to so brilliant and curious a world.

A group of his compatriots gathered round him; they were oddly out of place in the South Atlantic, for they had no clothes but those in which they had left their cities, and they all wore cloth caps, bought in the firm belief that a sea voyage demanded them. They seemed to have just stepped out of an office to visit a shop across the road.

'All the same,' said the chess-player, determined from now on to be a cynic, 'he is here to watch us.'

'To watch over us,' Mr Feitel corrected him dreamily. 'To watch over us.'

'He is not a police agent at all,' added Berta indignantly.

'But what did he come here for?' insisted the fat man with the lisp. 'Would you come down from the first-class for nothing? No! Would I? No! Would Berta? No! Why did he come here? Tell me that!'

He put his thumbs in the arm-holes of his vest, and walked two steps away and two steps back. For him, said his serious expression, there was logic, nothing but logic.

'I do not know,' Berta answered truthfully.

She was convinced, however, that she did know why he had returned again and again. She blushed. Mr Feitel saw her embarrassment unmoved. He had long since resigned himself to the fact that, while his friends commiserated with him on his daughter's thinness, she was devastatingly attractive to the Gentiles.

'What is he?' he asked.

'He doctors animals,' said Berta faintly.

'Animals! Do animals have doctors? What kind of animals?' asked the chess-player.

'Sheep,' answered Berta, waiting for the outburst of comment.

It came. When the hands had ceased to wave and the mouths to gabble, Mr Feitel murmured:

'He doctors sheep? So gentle, so humble that even sheep he cares for? My daughter, the man should be a Jew.'

'He is not,' said Berta.

'In the eyes of God he has a Jewish heart. Has any one of you seen prejudice in him? Has he ever shown that he shows a difference between Jew and Gentile?'

'No,' the fat man admitted. 'But he is a fool.'

'You have well said the man is a fool. To such God allows greatness and from such shall come deliverance,' said Mr Feitel impressively.

Danno Flynn appeared at the after end of the promenade deck. There was no immediate evidence of greatness in him, nor did he descend to them in a manner befitting the deliverer of Israel – for he slid down the rail of the ladder to the main deck – but he undeniably had an air, and he was not in the least put out by the eyes that, almost reverently, gazed at him.

'Sure and I knew me old cock would be on deck!' he exclaimed.

He seemed to slap Mr Feitel on the back, but his patient felt the hand alight firmly, gently, giving strength.

The chess-player moved his lips, rehearsing a speech that he had just composed in his school English; he considered that there were still too many mysteries unsolved.

'Pardon me, noble Mr Doctor, will you have the kindness to tell me please whether it is your purpose to practise in Brazil?'

''Tis not me purpose, 'tis the curse that is on me,' answered Danno. 'For, God help me, I am the biggest fool in Eire!'

Mr Feitel smiled benignly and began to talk to himself in a soft sing-song. Danno looked at him anxiously.

'Now be off with you!' he said, waving his arms at the little group as if they had been an obstinate herd of sheep. 'And let you not be troubling his reverence with your foreign talk and him with no strength to listen to his own!'

Mr Feitel's friends hastily moved on. The deck had become for them a street, with a person in authority to prohibit loitering.

Berta laughed.

'He is not light-headed,' she said. 'He is praying for you.'

24

''Tis very civil,' Danno answered. 'But he should be sleeping now.'

He stood behind the old gentleman's chair and gently stroked the prominent veins of his temples. In two minutes Mr Feitel was asleep.

'Why are you leaving your country if you did not have to?' Berta asked.

There was no longer any tone of cross-examination in her voice; she asked with the trust of a child that she would be answered.

''Twas like this, Biddy,' answered Danno. 'A little yellow man came to me house, and he telling me that he was spending a great fortune to raise sheep on the far mountains of Brazil, and begging me to work with him – for if the sheep didn't die on him, 'twas only because the ewes were barren. I will not, says I, for what would I be doing in India? 'Tis not India, he says, 'tis America. Then do you go to my uncle, says I, who is in Wyoming these thirty years and as good a man with the sheep as I am meself. So he told me 'twas South America and pressed a thousand pound into me hand, but I would not take it. Will ye come so far as Dublin with me, Mr Flynn, he asks. I will that, I said – for he was a friendly little yellow man and free with his money, God forgive him! And when we had drunk three parts of the whisky in Dublin, he would have me come to London and drink French wines. And how many days we were in London I misremember, but I signed me name on a paper and when the drink passed from me I found meself in a first-class cabin on the raging ocean, with all the money in the world in me pocket and a two-year contract.'

'But that is terrible! It's criminal!' she cried, all her pity for the exiled welling up.

'It was surely!' he laughed. 'But 'tis no fool that I am after all, for would not a man be glad to leave his country for a sight of your sweet face?'

'Then we'll comfort each other, Daniel,' she said frankly, linking her arm in his. 'There is only a week more before we land, but it shall be a happy week for us.'

'Let you not be talking so, Biddy!' cried Danno, much

shocked by the nearness of her and the openness of her speech. 'Would I be telling you of your eyes and your hair and the shape of you like a young tree and it heavy with fruit? And would I be kissing you in dark places till I was drunk with the scent of you and the white skin that is of a queen surely, and would I let you go then, and you the world's wonder and the love of my heart? I will not be parting from you and his reverence, I tell you. It's a poor bargain I have to offer you with no country of my own and no women to greet you in the street, saying – there goes the beauty that is the wife of Danno Flynn. But let you have patience for the two years, and you will not be lonely.'

'I will not, surely,' she answered, unconsciously falling into the lilt of his speech. 'But if I do not go with you I shall be lonely to the end of my days, and the women crying for pity of me.'

Firefly

I could not guess why he had so urgently insisted that I
should dine with him. To share our memories, he said. It
seemed most unlikely that any memories of mine could be
of value. The war had been over for two years and what
little I had known about the shady characters operating in
Bucharest in 1940 was out of date. If Rumanians, they were
probably dead; if British and more or less alive, they had
returned to their peacetime occupations.

It was still his job to gather information from Eastern
Europe. Today it would be fashionable to call him a Spy-
master. But in these early nineteen fifties we did not simplify
the paramilitary trades so coarsely and outright. However,
I suppose that even now I ought not to mention his name.
The rest can be told.

I had never known him show impatience in the old days.
But there in the restaurant he did, when the waiter delayed
his bill. He ordered me – almost – to come back with him
to his flat. We would have our coffee in peace, he said, and
shoved me into a taxi. As soon as we arrived, he switched
on his formidable radio. It was not a commercial job; it
had been constructed by someone who knew more about
electronics than cabinet-making.

The voice we heard was unmistakeable. It was the light
contralto of Firefly, travelling up the Wallachian rivers,
across the passes of the Carpathians and the Hungarian
plain, and over Vienna to his London flat still as clear as in
the Bucharest studio. So that was it. He wanted, I thought,
to talk about her. But even on that entrancing subject I had
little to contribute. He had been on far more intimate terms
with her than I was.

'You knew her,' he said, as if that were an unforgettable privilege. Well, in a way, it was.

'Only through you.'

'Yes, but you understood us both. Wasn't it you who told me that I must not try to take her home in a match box?'

I may have done so. If I did say something about collecting glow-worms in match boxes, it was not very profound. I merely meant that I couldn't see Firefly as a refugee in London, whoever paid her rent.

She came of a family of Transylvanian horse-dealers and was of pure Rumanian blood, bathed from birth in the folk music of her country. She belonged more to the concert hall than cabaret, though to look at her one would not think so. She dressed theatrically. It was not only her voice which she wanted admired. The wonder to me was that she ever had the resolute patience to become so great an artist.

Fragility had been my first impression of her. It was quite wrong. Though she was small-boned and delicate as any princess in a fairy tale, she was far too robust a character to be in need of care and protection. Her face, too, was small, eaten up by eyes. They were deep grey, intelligent eyes – spiritual, if you like, at any rate in the sense that I always felt her somewhat flashy outward appearance to be completely irrelevant.

Her contralto was clear as some full-throated bird outside the window, making a last passionate announcement of home and territory before going to roost. There were no primitive, gipsyish sobs and trills. The voice licked the atmosphere with little spurts of flame. I had a curious sense of watching it back across lost Europe into that unknown studio – watching it rather than hearing it.

He demanded that I should listen more carefully.

'Would you say she was happy?' he asked.

That seemed a damned silly question. I could no more tell from her voice whether she was or not than one can tell whether some whining pop singer is as miserable as he sounds. I replied that she was always happy.

'No! She was always gay. That's not the same thing. She was never content with herself. It stands to reason. She

28

couldn't have developed into what she is if she had not always been looking for something more to give.

I felt that he had become too emphatic and professional. His face, once bronzed by the Black Sea sun, now looked tired and white with two cavernous blue lines from nostrils to chin. Like some self-confident consultant he was too inclined to meet and hold my eyes. Challenge or analysis? Surely to God he couldn't be thinking of extracting Firefly to the West at this late date?

He had been fascinated by her, so far as he allowed himself time for such frivolities; but the attachment could hardly have survived four more years of war and two of uneasy peace. Anyway, from the young Firefly's point of view he had been little more than a devoted cavalier. She had at the bottom of her the Latin woman's impulse to fidelity. Certainly she made experiments – within reason – to find a lover worthy of it; but that is the privilege of any lovely woman with an adoring public.

'Do they treat her well?' I asked.

'*They*? They'd give her one of the old royal castles if she asked for it,' he replied. 'But that wouldn't account for the joy, the . . . well, fulfilment which I hear. Or think I hear.'

He mumbled that in the old days he had studied her voice, speaking or singing, every inflection, if only to suffer.

I may have been the first person to whom he had ever admitted that. Nobody ever suspected that he had been so overwhelmingly in love with her.

'Is she going to be married or something?' I asked.

'Perhaps. They are so perfectly suited to each other. But I doubt if she looks that far ahead. Or wants to.'

'Anyone I know?'

'No. But you would have heard of him,' he said. 'He was in gaol in our day. Mihai Vitalianu.'

Indeed I had heard of him. He was that most romantic of idealists, a boyar turned Tolstoyan revolutionary. If he wasn't in exile, he was in military confinement.

I also knew that Vitalianu had become a communist. Since he was more of a left-wing liberal than anything else, that was surprising. But under all his passionate principles he had a logical mind, and he must have seen that unless he joined the party he would merely be beating the air on behalf of his beloved peasants.

'I don't believe he'll stand his new creed very long,' I said.

'He hasn't stood it.'

'But he was near the top.'

'Yes. Dangerously near the top. And if he can carry the army with him he could be another Tito. He has gone too far to draw back. It has been win or lose for the last twenty-four hours.'

Firefly's voice made nonsense of fourteen hundred miles. We were in Bucharest, not London. Reception was perfect enough to hear the catch of her breath. She had never learned to breathe as a singer should, uninterested in packing reserves of air into a space already full of the pressure of genius. For the technique of Rumanian, Russian and Magyar songs it was not essential.

I asked him if he was in touch with Vitalianu.

'Not directly. I just know what is going on – the timing, the personalities. But there will be nothing to tell me who arrests and who gets arrested till the news is made public. And I must know before that.'

There was a break for a propaganda flash. Before giving out the rest of Firefly's programme, the announcer informed us that she was the world's most moving interpreter of folk music because she herself was a peasant. She was not. She was the privately educated child of a small capitalist. But the legend was more convenient.

'That's why I need you,' he went on. 'She can't hide her mood from me. If I can know that Vitalianu has failed as soon as she knows, there will be agents who'll have time to cover their tracks. It's so important that transmitters are standing by to warn them. But we must both be sure. All alone, I might not be – well, objective enough.'

I found his theory far-fetched. Unless she broke down in tears – which would be utterly unlike the Firefly I remembered – it was impossible to judge her mood.

No, it was not, he insisted, not if one had lived for the

voice. The outer mood of the entertainer could of course be simulated; the inner mood of the woman could not be. He assured me that any of Firefly's lovers – how he hated that plural! – could distinguish.

'But will Vitalianu tell her?'

'I used to know him very well. Yes, very well. It was through him that I first met her. When he returned from exile, both of them were often in my flat. I became the hopeless lover, straight out of Italian opera', he added ironically, more to himself than to me. 'He was such a brilliant, generous fellow. We knew then that war was inevitable. A peasant revolt might have been useful. Vitalianu was too young, but the only leader they would have followed.'

He lectured me on the mentality of traitors. Not the little ones. The real big shots with two loyalties. The kind that terrify governments with the mere thought that they might exist.

'Think of the strain on him!' he went on. 'Given his character, he must hate himself. There's no piece of himself that he can trust. So he would tell her the main issue. Not details. What would she want with details? But the sharing with her is essential to him. If he couldn't relax with her and trust her instinct, he'd lose patience, start taking reckless short cuts.'

He underlined Vitalianu's exhaustion at the end of his politician's day. Then he would go home to Firefly – his home or hers, with a discreet security agent outside the door – and hang up all his intricate deceptions with his hat. Those two must have been living month after month in that fever of heightened sympathy which the rest of us only experience on the last night before some parting which threatens to be for ever.

The programme ended. I seemed to hear from the echoing studio two light, rapid footsteps before synthetic applause covered the sound.

'She is impatient to be off,' he said. 'Vitalianu is waiting for her – if he is still about.'

That was gross sentimentalism on the doubtful evidence of two steps, and I said so.

31

'No, she's on twice every Wednesday,' he answered. 'She will sing again at one our time, eleven their time. Between the two shows they always dine together. That's the sort of useless little fact I do know. Confirmed by two reliable sources.'

'He would find time for her in a crisis?'

'If he were sure of army support and winning, he mightn't. But if he suspected it was his last chance to say goodbye – yes, he would find time.'

He switched the radio off and poured some drinks. Freed of the soft, excitable language, we were back in the world of commonsense geography without any duty to be present at that far-off supper table where the low, urgent voices of Firefly and Vitalianu spoke only for each other. We did not discuss them at all, looking the other way from delicacy, as it were.

Only once did he intrude. We were talking about the unavoidable conflict between economics and liberalism, when he suddenly remarked.

'There's no one else like Mihai Vitalianu.'

It fitted; but I suspect that he was not thinking of politics at all, that he meant that no one was so well suited as Firefly to be his consort.

'Better turn the damned thing on,' he muttered at last. 'They don't always run to schedule.'

We listened impatiently while a dance band played pre-war music. In some other studio Firefly and her gipsy fiddler, the cymbalo and the double bass were standing ready. The announcer, looking at her through his sound-proof window, failed to make his introduction long enough, or else she did not come in on her cue. There was a moment of complete silence.

She opened with a lingering, wavering cry and whipped from the top note straight into a song from the Banat of astonishing speed and vivacity. My companion sat up sharply and insisted that I must notice shrillness in the voice. I couldn't. I reminded him that he wanted me to tell him when his imagination was out of hand. The song called for excitement and she seemed to be acting it efficiently.

Perhaps she was not on full form, but I never appreciated her in music which showed Magyar influence. She was at her best when she tore the heart out of the Rumanian plains.

'You can't! There's no evidence!' I protested as his hand crawled over the edge of the table on which the telephone was standing.

'In a match box,' he answered. 'I wish I had! There is too much caution in us all. I *know* he's finished, I tell you!'

He tore at his long, white fingers as instinct struggled with common sense. There might be too much caution, but the head of a department didn't, couldn't ring the alarm along the Danube because a singer was off form. I could not deny that the flames were out, but that was all.

The next song was a *doina*. She started so artificially that I assumed she was bored and impatient to return to Vitalianu. Up to the middle of the first verse I could see that the expert, too, was doubting his theory.

And then, I suppose, in spite of her armour of blind misery, she realised what she was singing: a lament. It is a thing we have forgotten in the uniformity of our urban life. Lament. There will be a soldier here and there who knows what it means. He may have heard the cry of the bugle, over a lonely burial, follow the spirit into the sharp, foreign air, or listened to the 'Flowers of the Forest' while tears, unnoticed, spread over the grim face of the piper.

That was the quality of Firefly's *doina*, for she had found in it the expression of her agony. As the voice soared and wailed and broke, I heard – I was in no state to see anything – a meaningless string of code-words and code-names dictated into the telephone. They punctuated the terrible melody of grief, staccato as the sounds of men killing each other in the distance while still you stand by a grave.

Keep Walking

She strolled quickly away from the post box, knowing that the game was up. This was the end, and she was not prepared for it. She had always expected it to come – if it had to come – at home or in the course of some police check. But evidently they had not found out her name. They only knew about the post box and the timing. She would learn how they knew after her second or third interrogation. If she had then any curiosity left. There was nothing for it but to keep walking until those two security agents came alongside and gripped her arms.

The trick had worked for nearly a year. She posted her reports just before the box was cleared; the envelope would then be at the top or conspicuous among the top four or five. Thus it was easy for the postman to pocket and pass on the letter. One had only to be sure that the right man was on the collection round. It had even been possible, in an emergency, to by-pass the censorship of foreign mail.

She had not given herself away by any change of expression or sudden movement. She could count on that. After dropping the letter in the box she had continued on her way at an even pace. Behind her eyes remained a photograph of the scene. She had time to run it through memory and develop it as she walked.

On the opposite pavement, where usually there was only a handful of women scurrying home to prepare lunch, two men had been talking together. They were in no way remarkable. They might have been two door-to-door salesmen or canvassers comparing notes. It was the greatest luck that she knew one of them by sight; the most abominable luck that she had not spotted him before the letter was posted.

The photograph also showed two more men on her side of the street, looking in a shop window. They might be innocent passers-by but, if they were not, they fell neatly into the composition. One pair would wait until the collection was made from the box; the other pair would make the arrest.

She did not look round. She tried to believe herself a plain, respectable citizen so that neither her walk, her back nor her hands could possibly suggest guilt. Now, what would experienced police agents do? Their case could not yet be quite complete. It would be unshakeable as soon as that envelope at the top of the box was opened. But for the moment? Well, since their suspect appeared unworried and tripping along fairly purposefully, they would tail her; it might be profitable to find out where she was going and to whom she talked.

But they could take no risks of losing her. If she hailed a taxi or jumped on a bus, that would be the end. She could not be allowed to break contact. They would instantly obstruct any move which gave her the slightest chance of escaping.

So keep walking. A harmless human activity. She herself knew very well what a lot of evidence could be extracted from it. Tail a suspect who was walking, tail for an hour, and one could almost tell character, income, the working of digestion and the rising fears.

Her fears. God, it was difficult not to show any! Death was the least. Death was a companion just as present in her personal war as in any public one. What appalled her was the certainty that when at last she died she wouldn't be recognisable to herself in body or mind. Well, she had always accepted that. Why? The answer was something neutral for half her brain to think about while she kept walking. Patriotism? Democracy? More words! No one ever risked death for anything that couldn't be expressed in two syllables. Hatred. That was it.

Hardest of all was not to look round. If she did, they might arrest her at once. Her only chance of delaying the end was to show herself cleanly, absolutely unconscious that she was followed.

Having been trained herself in the secret police, she could imagine the messages going back to headquarters by walkie-talkie – or by telephone perhaps, if there were a third person who could leave the hunt to use it.

'We have got her,' they would say, 'but it's worthwhile finding out her name and where she is going. No, sir, no danger of losing her. She doesn't know. Couldn't know.'

Yes, they had to make certain that she was not merely returning to an office nor on any daily routine such as shopping or visiting a café. She very slightly quickened her pace, settling down, so far as pavement and people allowed, to a steady five-and-a-half kilometres an hour. She might be hurrying home, but, if she was, why not take her usual public transport instead of wearing out smart town shoes? So long as they were kept guessing, so long as they could not jump to any conclusion, they would follow.

Direction had been decided for her on leaving the post box. She must not change it too abruptly; she had to appear intent on something. Well, her present course would do. It led straight to the inner suburbs on the east of the city. After twenty minutes she thought it wise to offer them a little diversion. A taxi was approaching. She hesitated as if about to stop it. When the driver began to pull in, she shook her head and walked on. That would give them some conjectures to think about if they were still behind. Were they? She dared not find out. One single suggestion that she was suspicious, and they would no longer take the risk of losing her.

She wondered if they could tell that she was armed. That was not an urgent matter yet, nor likely to be. Still, it was worth a thought. Certainly they could be sure, after such long, detailed observation, if the gun had been in a shoulder holster or a pocket. She doubted, however, if an automatic nestling across the navel could be spotted from behind. They might reasonably assume that someone who might be searched would not be such a fool as to carry one. They would be on their guard of course, but not keeping the question continually in the forefront of consciousness. That might be important.

They had been following for six kilometres now, tiring and inclined to say to hell with the contact to whom she might be leading them. Their keen sense of duty, their strong instinct against running her in at once, ought to be revived. She decided to show more caution as if she were nearing her destination. It would be the first quick glance over her shoulder that they had seen, and therefore important. It would no longer be connected with the post box, left so far behind.

She looked round. She could not spot any followers at all. Had the walk and the discipline been all for nothing? Careful! That could not be assumed yet. She reminded her agonised feet of what was going to happen to them if she allowed herself to be too confident.

She chose a long residential street. There were very few pedestrians. If the hunters were still determined to take no action and stick to the trail, they would have to be very careful. However casual they appeared, they were bound to be out of place and conspicuous. Her experience had taught her how they – if they existed – would arrange that one. It was going to show how relentless the pursuit really was. If they knew their job (and no one knew it better) there ought to be a car moving more or less on parallel lines. As soon as her two shadows were forced to fall too far behind, they would signal the car to take over.

She spotted the car. It drove past in the same direction and parked on the other side of the road. She could not really have said why she was certain it was the car. Perhaps because it did exactly what it should, covering the road she was in and two side streets into which she might turn; perhaps because nobody opened the door at which the driver was ringing or pretending to ring; perhaps the instinct of the hunted.

It was oddly comforting to get her fear back. Now she knew that she had not imagined they were after her. Also she had proof that so far she had decoyed them into believing her movements significant. That report collected from the post box must already have been read. Her guilt was beyond question. Yet they still thought it worthwhile to see where she was going before they struck.

She continued eastwards. She was now passing through a local shopping centre, and the two could safely close up. She longed to confirm that they were still on her trail, but every trick she knew for seeing who was behind her was equally well known to them. Show absolute unconcern, and they would wait. Keep walking, and they had to know the reason why. The view of her steadily moving back must be beginning to hypnotise them.

All the same it was tempting to make a dash for it. Through a house or shop? Into a back garden? The bushes of a park? But she hadn't a hope and knew it. There would always be a car or two on that parallel course and uniformed police somewhere in the background.

Nearly two hours now. Ten kilometres more or less. To do more in a straight line might not be convincing. They would accept it as normal that she should not take a taxi all the way to her rendezvous, but why not take one part of the way? The weary conversation behind her must have become a debate, one of them in favour of picking her up without delay, the other protesting against such a waste of the long grind.

So it was time for another sweetener. She looked at her watch and began to stroll more gently. Round two blocks and back to her starting point. She saw the car again. That was careless of them. It confirmed that they had never detected any hint that she was on her guard.

Again she looked at her watch and made a gesture of impatience, hardly perceptible but they wouldn't miss it. She started to stride out at a good six kilometres an hour towards the outskirts of the city, and allowed that hypnotising back view of her to show some anxiety.

She knew where she was going and when she meant to arrive. There might be a hope, just a slight hope, if the same two obstinate men continued on the job. Probably they would. After all their trouble, they would ask permission to carry on. Headquarters would be very impressed indeed if they could follow their suspect across the whole city and out of it and discover her contact in the end. There was little point in substituting fresh agents for the two who by now were familiar with her character.

The real difficulty was not these two, but their unknown colleagues. The field. The rest of the hunt. Some occupation must be found to delay them. There was a newspaper seller ahead on the other side of the road. That would do. A shop would not. If she entered any sort of shop, it would break the spell. She crossed the road, bought two papers almost without slowing her stride and walked straight on, feeling sorry for the newsvendor who was sure to be investigated in case more than a coin had passed between them.

She rolled the papers up as she walked, but had trouble in keeping them rolled. She needed two rubber bands or strips of gummed paper. She hadn't got either. A couple of stamps were the only available means. And who the devil would take something from a handbag and stick it on rolled newspapers without stopping? Well, but she must not stop, not on any account. They would have to work it out for themselves. Perhaps she was in a tearing hurry. Perhaps it was all a part of some new, interesting technique which would fascinate their curiosity.

She kept walking, holding a rolled paper in each hand until the gum was safely dry. She knew what she wanted: a high fence or wall. In that district of builders' yards and small workshops it should not be hard to find. She saw the proper setting at last, up a turning to the right. There was a big printing works on one side, small houses on the other. She turned sharply into the street, threw one of the news-papers over the printer's wall and walked on. As soon as the two turned the corner and took up the trail, they wouldn't miss the obvious inference that one paper had gone over the wall and that the other was still to be delivered.

By God, no, she wouldn't be arrested now! She was really worth following. Especially since the printer happened to be a government printer. The newspaper would – presumably – be easily found, but what had been rolled up in it and who had picked it up? That unfortunate printing works was going to be turned inside out. She reckoned that the whole of the team would be instantly and urgently occupied except for her two followers. They were committed to her so long as their boots and feet held out.

She was clear of the inner suburbs and among the factories. The main avenue was landscaped, bordered by lawns and imposing offices. Behind it were the service roads, the waste lots, the dumps, the uninviting cafés. She looked at her watch, on this occasion because she really wanted to know the time. It was going to be a close thing, but she must not hurry.

Keeping her even, persuasive pace, she turned off the avenue into the worst stretch of all, empty and far too long. Surely they must realise what was going to happen and arrest her now? She imagined she heard their footsteps closing up, but dared not look back or run.

The third corner was a possible. Far from perfect, but all the chance she was ever going to get. She shot round it and crouched behind a lump of concrete, once part of a weighbridge and now standing shapeless among thistles. There were a few workers further along the road, all busily occupied with brooms or vehicles or last-minute loading.

The two followed almost at once without any precautions at all, startled out of their trance by her sudden evasion just as she hoped they would be. They were still the same pair, seen once near the post box two-and-a-half hours earlier. Hurrying to restore the broken contact, they passed within two yards of her silenced gun with their eyes fixed ahead on the parked vehicles and the factory gate. She let them pass. It had not been her intention, but why take an unnecessary risk? Lucky for them that they had panicked and tried to catch up instead of searching the corner itself.

The factory clock struck six. Cars, bicycles and pedestrians surged out of the gate and surrounded them. She saw them trying, she thought, to give orders to the mixed and flowing column. She wrapped her head in her sweat-soaked scarf, turned her coat inside out and ripped the heels off her shoes so that neither her height nor her bearing would be familiar to her followers if they were in any position to pick out individuals. At last she could allow herself to appear as tired as she felt, shuffling along in a bunch of fellow workers like a weary factory hand twice her age.

She kept walking, now no longer alone, until she saw a bus ready to start. Where it went was unimportant; for her its destination was freedom. Her name was still unknown and her papers in perfect order. After a few professional, quite simple changes in her appearance she could cross the frontier.

Yours Obediently

They all wanted to do something for Mr Melman – the Major especially – though suggestions when discussed seemed more in the nature of persuading him to do something for them. That was reasonable enough. The obvious and most valuable way to befriend a newcomer was to give him an active interest in the community.

Mr Melman was not a recluse but lived quietly. When he first arrived his manner at once attracted the pious and perplexed, for he was very ready with words of comfort. Tolerance, melancholy, a sort of watchful kindliness – all those were stamped into his worn, dark face. The Major wondered if he had not in the past been affected by some oriental creed of renunciation. He kept this surmise to himself. Long experience had taught him that the play of imagination, unless one had a more than military command of words, was usually misunderstood.

The village naturally was curious. A passive curiosity. Mr Melman was known to have lived abroad as some minor official in the Colonial Service, and that was enough. So many of the little houses of main street and square had been purchased by unknown Londoners: schoolmasters, journalists, small businessmen who had made sufficient money to retire. The past of any of the newcomers was therefore irrelevant, belonging to a wider world. Curiosity confined itself to the odder daily happenings of the present.

Melman's gentle firmness in the affair of the vicar's dog had impressed everyone. The dog was nearly blind with age but still preserved its youthful habit of taking chances in crossing the village street. The screech of brakes had undoubtedly enhanced its estimate of its own importance. Punishment was the worst possible: paralysed at one end and normal enough at the other to lick bewilderedly its master's hand. The vet was away. The vicar was distraught. The Major, to his own shame, found himself dithering. It was Melman, his face motionless, his eyes pitying, who placed the dog under the decent cover of the churchyard wall and borrowed the Major's gun.

'I am sorry,' said the Major, walking home with him. 'I am very sorry. I shouldn't have let you. But you were the only one of us who was calm.'

'I was glad to be of assistance. And I quite understand. I have noticed before, Major, that soldiers are very sensitive.'

'What's surprising about that?'

'Well, ending life . . .' Mr Melman murmured with a delicacy which seemed to the Major unnecessary.

'Oh, I see! I've thought a lot about that. Put it this way! A man is prepared to die for what he believes in – country, regiment or just his unit. But it does nobody any good if he simply throws his life away. So that means – bluntly – that he must kill before he's killed. Morally wrong perhaps, but it feels natural enough when you're in it and excited.'

'I'm sure you are right, Major,' Melman said. 'But I can't imagine myself finding any excitement.'

Towards such a man the Major was protective. He prized a sense of duty and could spot it when he saw it. He had no doubt at all that Melman, as a civil servant, had carried out orders promptly and to the best of his ability. That picture fitted a police sergeant rather than a grave comforter, but was all the more reason for respecting Melman's privacy.

'If you took the trouble to draw that man out,' his wife had insisted, 'you don't know what you might find.'

Well, that at least was undeniable, though she herself had failed to get anything out of Melman but reserved, conscientious politeness. Women, the Major often thought, preferred life to resemble a pond into which they could throw stones; they liked to take from and give to an ever-expanding circle regardless of the consequences. But one saved a lot of trouble by leaving ponds alone until such time as an appeal came in to drain, clean or renovate, when one

43

accepted duty to the neighbour and did as much over as could secretly be managed.

So, continually pressed to do more than lean on Melman's garden gate and talk genially about the weather, he compelled himself to venture a more personal approach.

'Ever thought of standing for the Rural District Council?'

'I couldn't make a speech, Major.'

'Anybody can. All you need to make a speech is an opinion. It runs away with you. Before you know it, you've made a speech.'

'I wouldn't feel strongly enough. There are always two sides to every question.'

'That's useful, too,' the Major persisted. 'You could lay off the local politics and help everyone with administration.'

Indeed he could. He seemed to be perfectly at home among government forms and was always willing to help the shy or the ignorant with their claims for benefits, licences and pensions. It had naturally been the widows and spinsters of his own age who first came to the kind Mr Melman for advice, but word had quickly spread of his ability to fill in blank spaces with ease and authority.

He lived alone, and on two or three evenings a week came down to the pub for a social drink. He liked to be invited to join in any game but never played with exclamations or vivacity. At darts he was so solemnly accurate that Fred Emerson, who kept the pub, suggested on impulse that he might captain the local team; what the youngsters needed to win their away matches was a responsible person in charge of them. But on second thoughts, Emerson said, he was glad when Melman refused.

'It wouldn't do for them all to come home too early, Major,' he added.

The Major saw what he meant. Melman was a very possible captain. He said the right things and smiled at the right jokes. His jollity was no more artificial than that of many other serious-minded neighbours, but they did give a bit of themselves with it. Melman was too noticeably limited to what was expected of him.

'A very reliable fellow,' the Major insisted. 'All those

women who think he's a kind of ministering angel have got him wrong.'

'Sometimes I think he could have been in old Efford's trade,' Fred remarked.

Again the Major understood. Efford was the local funeral director and highly respected on the job or off it. He had a healthy, mediaeval attitude to death. He made all the time-honoured jests with the doctors, and they with him. Efford was a deeply religious man who saw himself as the disposer of something so unimportant that he could – when not on duty – laugh at it.

But there was no resemblance between so richly charged a character and Melman who, though a church-goer, probably saw attendance as a parade: a service like any other service, the reasons for which were not his business. So much was not his business. His life of retirement followed a narrow track. Whatever appeared on it he treated with kindness; what was off to each side of the line he ignored.

Mere conjecture. The Major knew it was mere conjecture and likely to be unfair. Yet it was odd how often this searching for the essence of a man had its uses. One had a reasonable intelligence report to give, right or wrong, when somebody called for it.

It was the vicar who called for it. A new churchwarden would be needed. Did the Major think that Mr Melman would do?

'Well, so long as you realise what you're in for,' said the Major cautiously. 'He reminds me a little of a sergeant-major in my orderly room. All the evidence for and against the accused was neatly and fairly presented. But if the Military Police had run him in, he was guilty.'

'I don't think Melman is like that,' the vicar protested. 'I was much impressed by his gentleness on that . . . that sad occasion, and I blame myself for ever thinking he was cold. Besides, one sees how the children love him.'

They didn't. They treated him as an animated slot machine. The Major, however, was too good-natured to say so. Mr Melman lived in a pretty white-and-yellow cottage on a lane which was used by a dozen children on their way to school. At that hour – for he was an early riser – he was generally to be seen trimming his neat privet hedge or digging the kitchen garden. The children were inclined to stop and inspect him very warily over the hedge. When they did, he was quick and eager to distribute sweets. That was the idyllic picture to which the vicar referred, but the Major doubted if any real affection was in it. To stare at Melman was cheaper than dropping a coin in a machine and nearly as dependable.

'The point is: do *you* like him?' the Major asked.

'Yes. Oh, yes! I would call him a dedicated man in a curious way – so dedicated that he treats me as if I were some sort of official. I suppose I am, though I hope there is more to it than that.'

'Well, we mustn't press him too hard. He has a right to his peace. I expect he got as tired of doing his duty as the rest of us.'

'But would you sound him? You know him better than anyone.'

Better than anyone? The Major was well aware that he knew nothing of him. But it was at least evident that he and Melman treated each other with respect. That was perhaps how the myth of understanding had grown.

Rather unwillingly he tackled him over the usual garden gate, reassuring himself by the thought that the job of churchwarden would relieve Melman's loneliness, whatever effect he was likely to have on the vicar. He was unaccountably relieved, like Fred Emerson, when the man showed no eagerness.

'If you tell me I should . . .' Melman began.

'It might suit you. I don't know. But if you want me to ask you to take it on – well, I've no right to say you should.'

'As good as anyone's, Major. Obedience – that's what I understand. It helps one to get accustomed to one's duty. It's like what you were saying the other day about killing in war.'

'Obedience is no excuse at all. Nothing to do with it!' the Major exclaimed, and then, feeling that he had been unwarrantably brusque, added: 'I'll tell you a thing I've never told anyone. I had to supervise an execution once. Unofficial, but I obeyed. We shot him in the back of the neck. Didn't do it myself, but I can't get out of it that way. We is we, if you see what I mean.

'I've no objection to capital punishment in principle. None at all! A very useful deterrent! Nine times out of ten the world is better without the man who is executed. Those damned professional liberals have got the argument all wrong. The State has every right to take life. What it doesn't have is the right to order somebody to take it. And whether you hang or press a button or shoot, a human hand has to do it. I won't have that. Society has no right to demand it. Killing in cold blood is murder of the soul which kills.'

To the Major's surprise, Mr Melman for the first time strongly disagreed with him.

'You're wrong about that,' he said. 'Now, strictly between ourselves – you always take me just as I am, Major, and I know I can trust you – strictly between ourselves, I was the official hangman. It's a police job like any other. And I don't think it has made any difference to me at all.'

Women's Lib

Wasn't there some old Greek tragedy in which a band of women tore a civil authority into small pieces because he had no gold braid on his cap? I'm pretty sure that the Ancient Greeks did not wear official caps, but the principle is the same. Ever since 1926 I can never forget that under those appealing faces lurks a profound contempt for the opposite sex.

Perhaps it was nearer the surface then than now. There were still quite a lot of virgins about, and their dreams were of marriage and a home of their own. For the inadequately educated girl few other dreams had a hope of fulfilment; professions, black-coated or brass-hatted, were all out of her reach. No wonder she had a latent, feline resentment of the pretensions of the male.

Why do I choose 1926, you ask. Because that was the year of the General Strike and a call for volunteers to man the public services. Among the misty memories of hundreds of old Londoners will be one of a giant: of a 4–4–0 Great Western locomotive stopped two yards from the mouth of the east-bound tunnel in Earl's Court station. At a platform meant for trains of the District Line skittering like mice from one hole to another was this great, green monster which had never moved without space and due ceremony. The arch against which it would have been driven, had the six-foot driving wheels made half a revolution more, was lower than the boiler. This was before the rebuilding of the station and the approach from the west was open.

I was the guard of the empty train behind the engine. I had volunteered to wheel hand-trucks about as a porter, but when I ran into an old schoolfellow on Paddington station he appointed me to be his guard. Jimmy Fell was a railway engineer on leave from the wilds of Africa. He had been working with black labour a year or two longer than was good for him and felt imperial. He once abandoned me in the Exeter station buffet and I only found my own train because an amateur shunter had run him into the engine sheds by mistake.

He had driven all kinds of locomotive in his time, so the Great Western gave him a mainline express and the *County of London* to pull it. He treated her as his own pet car, and when he wasn't on the foot-plate he was wandering about inside her guts like Jonah with an oilcan. I call it an express, but all the signals were permanently at danger and we used to feel our way down to Devon from block to block, stopping to negotiate with other speculative railwaymen whenever we seemed to be on a line where we had no right.

After ten days or so of this, the Company chose us to take an excursion to Pangbourne. Yes, they actually wasted time on an excursion. It was a gesture, you see. Sir John Hardy always gave the saleswomen of his suburban branches an outing in the same week of June and, being proprietor of Models Ltd and on the board of the Great Western as well, was determined upon Business as Usual. The nation was paralysed, but he wouldn't disappoint his 'girlies' as he called them.

Well, the Great Western were moved by this touching faith in their organisation, so they agreed to the excursion. Britain with her Back to the Wall. They ordered the line to be cleared to Pangbourne and at 10.30 a.m. we pulled out of Paddington with the trustworthy Jimmy Fell at the levers and four full coachloads of chattering girlies between myself and him. Sir John and his managers naturally went by car. Their lives were of value.

We reached Pangbourne about midday. Our average of twenty-five miles an hour was excellent considering that Jimmy had climbed down twice to see which way the points were set and had been grazed by half a brick that was meant for the fireman. We never had the slightest trouble with the strikers – we were free entertainment for dull days – but our fireman thought he was entitled to call them names which would earn him half a brick at any time. He was a sort of fascist – or whatever they labelled themselves in those days – and all out to smash the reds. In private he sold silk stockings from door to door and he was hungry for any job that called for more muscle but just as little brain. He used to splash himself with oil and coal dust to look like a real fireman. He didn't. You might have taken him for a tramp who had been sheltering from the rain in a garage pit.

The girlies skipped off to a tent by the river to hear Hardy's annual speech and put away some lunch. Flags waved gaily over the white canvas and a little brass band played a welcome of the latest popular songs. It was a blazing June day with thunder in the air and when we had run the train into a siding we ourselves went to the local pub for beer and sandwiches. The bar had a few jokes at our expense – four coaches of women among three men and so forth. We didn't think them very funny, for there was something unnatural about those two hundred female passengers, the old catching the giggles from the young. We were uneasy as if there had been a wagon load of explosives just behind the engine. Perfectly safe, of course. But one is appalled by sheer quantity.

At three o'clock we went to work again. At first sight the task of getting the train from the down to the up line with the *County of London* at the right end appeared nearly hopeless; but Jimmy was a positive chap with a commanding manner, ready to take responsibility. An invaluable quality in Africa, I expect. He ran the Holyhead boat train into the only other siding, blocked a down freight, borrowed its locomotive and by occupying most of the main line between Pangbourne and Reading had hitched his *County of London* to the front of his own train. The girlies encouraged us with cheers and laughter, lined up on the platform and singing all the songs played by the band. They were tousled and shrill and the cheap make-up sold by Models Ltd was running in the heat.

While they climbed into the coaches, Sir John, who had been watching our manoeuvres with a sightseer's interest and a large glass of port, paced up the platform and made a little speech to Jimmy on his patriotism and what-not, shaking his hand with genial condescension. He mistook the fireman for the real article and congratulated him on not being led away by subversive and anti-Christian agitators. He made his money, I believe, in Australia where a strike's a strike and could not be expected to know that English labour leaders were more likely to be fervid chapel-goers than Marxists.

When this moving ceremony was over and the doors were shut and Sir John and his managers waving goodbye till next year, the *County of London* whistled and drew out of the platform in smart mainline style. I just had time to wave the green flag and blow my own little whistle, but I doubt if anybody was taken in.

Before we were fairly out of the station Jimmy stopped with such a jerk that an empty oil drum charged down the guard's van towards London by itself. I looked out of the window. A down train was creeping at us on the up line. We had forgotten one set of points after all our shunting, and the new arrival was proceeding with caution in search of authority.

While Jimmy and his vis-à-vis straightened matters out, the girlies flowed back onto the empty platform and began to dance. There was a lot of horseplay and shrieking, for they had the place to themselves. Sir John and his henchmen had left, and I kept discreetly to my van. I don't know if you have noticed that young women, by the mere fact of being in a group and unrestricted, can reach a state of innocent excitement that would take the ordinary man three or four double whiskies on an empty stomach.

The intrusive train passed on its correct line, and Jimmy and the fireman returned to the locomotive. I shepherded the girlies back into their compartments and walked down the train shutting doors and turning handles. We were forbidden to start till all handles were in a horizontal position. A strict rule. Even Jimmy observed it.

When I was halfway down the last coach I heard giggles

51

behind me and turned round. The passengers had opened the doors again.

'Now then, young ladies!' I said.

I thought my voice had just the right note of tolerant authority. They thought so, too. They thought I was perfect in the part. One of the girlies hollered:

'Ooh! Ain't 'e a duck!

I trotted back up the train with proper brisk officiousness and shut the doors. They fell in with my absurd wishes. There was no question of a struggle with door handles or direct disobedience; but just as soon as I was a dozen compartments up, the doors began to open behind me – one at a time, as neatly as a line of poppers bursting open from the bottom when you've nearly done them up to the top.

I stood by the locomotive wondering what a guard did next. Hitherto my job had been easy. I had to manhandle the contents of the van, check the waybills, brake whenever I got an S.O.S. from Jimmy and sometimes inspect tickets. With the ordinary mixed bag of passengers points of discipline did not arise and I was accustomed to think myself as good a guard as another. But now I was conscious of being a plain chap in flannel trousers and a sports coat.

Jimmy said I lacked character. He put his driver's cap on the side of his head and walked down the platform. He was lean, brown and clean-shaven, a maiden's dream born and fashioned for a uniform. The overalls of an engine driver were not, however, the right uniform; he looked too much like a film star in a stirring drama of life on the rolling rail.

'Ladies,' he appealed, mounting a luggage barrow, 'you've been given a nice day and we have to go back to London. Now be sensible and don't behave like babies!'

'A-oh bybies!' protested a voice, half-yearning, half-insulted.

Somebody else started a first-class imitation of a baby crying and they all joined in. You never heard such a row. Then they chose to regard Jimmy as the baby (for he was eminently motherable) and the more excitable spirits leaned out of the windows and made gestures of maternity at him.

Jimmy turned white and strolled – yes, strolled – back to the *County of London*. I think they must teach administrators of the African Empire a special walk for the casual entering of cannibal villages. He started the train. They were all safely inside and shut the doors themselves as soon as we gathered speed.

At Reading the staff of the junction had forgotten the existence of the excursion, and we were held up. But Jimmy didn't stop. He thundered slowly ahead at walking pace and occasionally, if it seemed likely there might be an obstacle, he reversed, keeping his beloved engine plunging back and forth as if he had been a dutiful gigolo guiding his grand-mother through a crowded ballroom. The girlies stuck their heads out and yelled encouragement but didn't dare to step out on platform or line.

Once clear of Reading we ran along with professional smoothness. There was no indiscipline except on the part of one young woman who tried to work her way along the footboard to the guard's van. I spotted her in time, and didn't try any 'dear young lady' on her. I opened fire with a paperweight and shouted that if she didn't get back into the train I should aim to hit next time. That worked. But my civil authority had gone. We normally obey a bus conductor or a guard or any honest fellow with braid on his cap just as unthinkingly as sheep a dog, but the moment his authority is tested it ceases to exist and passes to the armed forces of the Crown – or to a paperweight.

At Maidenhead we had to stop; some damned fools were marshalling a milk train and had tied up the line. The girlies flooded out onto the station and started to dance. No passengers were about, only the usual skeleton staff of amateurs. The excitement was still spontaneous, much too spontaneous, but its direction seemed to have been taken over by one Rhoda as ringleader – a magnificent creature, loudly dressed with the luxurious figure of a roly-poly angel sitting on a cloud, but the face, I tell you, of an ageless mule. Lord, how she must have despised men! Unaccountably cold and conceited she must have thought us.

Led by Rhoda, those sales ladies cleaned up the station.

They formed into clusters and played ring-a-ring-a-roses around every defenceless man on the platform until the whole lot had sheepishly taken refuge in the ticket office. They didn't run, you understand; they just drifted away on business and found that business, as it might be accidentally, behind a door that could be locked. You know the feeling of being followed through a field by a large herd of trotting bullocks. You don't run away, but you do climb the nearest gate rather than the farthest.

Jimmy and the fireman took refuge in noise and fog, making the *County of London* spout steam from its private parts. I can't tell you the mechanics of the process, but he caused it to throb and rejoice in its strength, pawing the lines and crying 'Hah' like the war-horse in Job. The girlies kept at a respectful distance. As for me, I climbed down to the track and watched through the intervals between the coaches. Whenever I caught a predatory female eye I started to tap at the wheels with a hammer. They left me alone feeling, I suppose, that I knew what I was doing and that it was necessary to their journey.

Up to this point it had been all clean fun. Men do, after all, arouse a certain pity in the female breast along with the contempt. Since they so obviously had the upper hand they would have been quite content to treat us with good-humoured scorn if an official of their own sex had not interfered. She was the amateur ticket-office clerk, and I imagine she had been calling those male colleagues who kept drifting into the office on improbable excuses a bunch of incompetent cowards. At any rate she was a woman of character and she was having no nonsense on her station. She marched out to deal with this impertinent excursion and began to round up the girlies with all the efficiency of a games mistress in her playing field. At that I began to tap my wheels more industriously than ever. When I thought it safe to look up again, Rhoda had crowned her with a fire-bucket and she was quietly crying in a puddle of water. The girlies paid no further attention to her. They were busy smashing the slot machines and helping themselves to chocolate.

This was going too far. I shouted 'All aboard!' waved my flag and blew a blast on the whistle. The line was not clear, but Jimmy caught on and put up a convincing show of a train just about to leave. The great driving wheels began to move and the artificial fog was shattered by one colossal whoosh of steam.

They were just piling into the compartments when Rhoda spoiled the picture.

'You stay there, mister,' she carolled. 'We'll get in when we're bloody well ready.'

That called our bluff of course. We couldn't start without them – or rather it had not yet occurred to us that we could.

It was then that our fireman lost his temper. His disdain for Jimmy and myself had been growing; after all he had been shooed away from doors by busy housewives throughout the suburbs whereas Jimmy had only to overawe a cheerful gang of black railwaymen. He got down from the footplate and walked along the platform, wiping his hands on a sodden yard of oily cotton waste. A horrid weapon against best frocks in a rough-and-tumble.

'Get on in, you silly bitches!' he roared.

His cave-man stuff damn near worked. The girlies were so startled that they began to get into the train. His silk stockings had taught him one of the elementary facts about women.

'Come on, Ma!' he ordered Rhoda, who was rather hesitantly standing her ground.

She was only about nineteen and that 'Ma' infuriated her. It struck her right on the secret sore of her spirit. She snatched his oily rag and wiped his face with it.

That was the detonator in the wagon of gelignite. It exploded. All the worry about fathers and brothers and sweethearts on strike, all the year spent behind counters controlling their natural instincts to be rude to customers who were rude to them, all was released in one blast of females over that fireman. Before we could get up to the rescue they had dragged him into a compartment. They were screaming with rage. I suppose the only people who hear that sound are the officials of a women's prison. There

55

was no doubt that the fireman would be for it if we couldn't pull him out.

It was no good calling for police; there weren't any. We dived under the train and opened the door which gave on to the tracks. The fireman's legs were poking out from cascades of loosened hair and still waving feebly. We took a leg each and heaved, and he came out leaving his jacket and shirt behind. On our rush to the engine his trousers dropped off him – not round his ankles, I mean, but vanished, disintegrated.

When we were all safely on the footplate, Jimmy opened up his steam screen to throw off the pursuit and we started. This time there was no bluff for them to call. They appreciated that we were running for our lives and didn't care how many of them were left behind. So far as I could see, they all managed to come aboard. I wiped the worst of the bloodstains and muck off the fireman and dressed him in Jimmy's spare overalls. He had only lost shreds of skin from his scalp and all his members were present and correct. He gibbered a bit, as was not unnatural, and kept grabbing at me.

'I'm not stopping till we get to police,' said Jimmy, setting his jaw.

I agreed with him. Anything was better than loosing our four hysterical coachloads into a London unprotected.

Jimmy had the *County of London* pounding along at a steady forty. It was risky but we had the mainline to ourselves and could see a mile ahead. Maidenhead had held us up quarter of an hour longer than was necessary. All went well till we were just outside Ealing. There our faithful engine took a horrible lurch to starboard and nearly flung us off the footplate. By the time Jimmy had jammed on the brakes and cut the speed down to ten miles an hour, we were careering through a goods yard surrounded by acres and acres of trucks. We could now hear the turmoil in the coach next to the engine. Somewhere they were still singing songs; somewhere they were shrieking with alarm; somewhere they were yelling foul abuse at the driver and his mates.

Our line was clear. Lord knows for what mysterious traffic the points had been set. Once we were in a cutting between houses where the rails were rusty with disuse and once running alongside a racecourse of District lines, all of them electrified. The *County of London* was bouncing like a dinghy in a tide-rip. She squealed, rocking round switch-back curves. I could see that Jimmy was in agony, for he loved that locomotive and the driving of it, but a look at the fireman was enough to keep us going.

We must have been dodging through the inner suburbs for a good ten minutes when we staggered over an incredible cluster of points and saw a deserted station ahead of us.

'Royal Oak?' Jimmy asked, as if he had just sighted the coast of America.

'Must be,' I answered confidently.

Of course that was absurd. When you are running into Paddington on a fast express Ealing and Royal Oak go by in two flashes; but we hadn't the faintest notion where we were, and it never occurred to us that we had left the Great Western system altogether for outer space. We decided that we had merely taken a very roundabout route to Royal Oak and we blessed that route since Paddington and whole posses of police could be only two minutes away.

Jimmy opened her out a little, and it was then that we saw a modest notice of EARL'S COURT and the mouth of the east-bound tunnel. We managed to stop a matter of two yards from it and made one collective jump for the stairs dragging the fireman between us. We were away before the terrors behind us could do more than half open the doors.

I heard that when the strike was over the *County of London* could not be returned to her home without a crane and a breakdown gang. The professional railwaymen said it was impossible to drive a 4–4–0 locomotive round those curves. I dare say it is. I swear the leading bogey jumped the track once and then bounced back again.

What happened to the girlies? Demurely working at the counters of Models Ltd, I suppose. But in my opinion it was no coincidence that next week the railwaymen were so horrified by anarchy that they voted to return to work.

Debt of Honour

It was not the nature of the Bagai to weep. Their training, like that of the district commissioner now standing by the loaded lorry which was to take him from them to the coast, forbade the expression of emotion in public. Dark eyes stared over the deep-breathing line of the giraffe-hide shields. The district commissioner stared back without a word. To a stranger it would have seemed that the Bagai were parting with their most hated enemy, for he would have known nothing of the long councils, the swearings of blood brotherhood, the agony of old men who had come alone and in the night to the beloved tent, terrified for their people's future in a changing and hostile world, as children whose father should be compelled, without hope of return, to leave them.

Overhead the clouds wallowed lazily up from the Indian Ocean, rolling westward through the grey morning like a herd of leisurely Bagai cattle towards the Bagai hills. The faint, deep lowing of thunder echoed from the edge of the escarpment where the spears of sun, radiant as in the steel engraving of some family Bible, pierced through a screen of straight-falling rain. To north and south the clouds were spreading into the heart of Africa without shedding any of their burden upon farms of white men and parched clearings of black. It was the copper-coloured Bagai who had all the luck.

The warriors, their backs towards their country and the long-needed rain, paid no heed to this good fortune. At such a crisis in the little nation's life, pasture and crops were irrelevant. Grief – collective, overwhelming grief – obsessed them. Yet their only gesture of farewell was the silent stare, answered, and for the same Spartan reasons, by the lonely

58

man standing at the side of his lorry. They had no royal salute with which to send Mark Lee-Armour on his way, for they had no kings. No slaying of men or cattle could appease their sorrow, for they had no tradition of sacrifice.

The two officials, one of State and one of Church, who accompanied Lee-Armour effaced themselves from the scene so far as dignity permitted, standing apart from the austere leave-taking with the delicacy of those who are present at a friend's parting from his beloved wife. One was the new district commissioner of the Bagai; the other was the Archdeacon of the Sultanates who had been on tour through the diocese and was seizing the opportunity of Lee-Armour's departure to travel down with him to the coast.

The vigil of grief ended, sharply and by almost telepathic consent between Mark Lee-Armour and his Bagai. He climbed into the cab of the loaded lorry and drove off. The new district commissioner, after a few halting words of promise and sympathy to the Bagai, mounted his pony and rode away. The archdeacon's black and gaudy driver followed the lorry, playing hosannas on his horn; he wore a clerical collar, as self-chosen badge of office, above the open neck of his yellow shirt, and he despised the uncivilised. The warriors themselves stood still, eyes raised to the mist of dust that hung, until it merged with the westward-flowing clouds, above the narrow road of rammed mud.

The archdeacon watched the swaying, uncompromising back of the lorry, a blind wall against farewells, and envied this departing district commissioner his life of devoted service to the neighbour. It was the life for which he himself, with half his being, had longed as a young man. The other half, however, had demanded from him a still higher service. Africa had happily integrated the two.

He was of the caste of the colonial officials, of their dress – at any rate when on tour – and even of their build except for a slight ecclesiastical portliness; but unlike these younger sons of empire, he had no material need to make a career in Africa. Even the missionaries had to admit – however strictly they preserved their charity for their converts – that a man of his fortune and family who had chosen a droughty diocese of three million square miles rather than the fat lawns of an English cathedral close could not be wholly worldly. They were also glad – and glad the archdeacon, too – that his cheque-book was wide open as any apostle's moneybag.

He had looked forward to the journey. To pass three days and nights in sole company with greatness would be a memorable experience. Yet when the sun had gone down and the scrub thorn around the camp was black lace against a crimson sky, the confiding dusk was full of disappointment. Lee-Armour never came out of the shadows. In a physical sense, as well, that was true. He followed as any shy animal the pattern and contours of darkness, and after supper – an unrevealing interlude as well-bred as any formal dinner party – while they sat and smoked by the fire, his face was always half-obscured by the straight column of smoke or caught at evasive angles by any sudden spurt of flame. The archdeacon assumed that the cause of this reserve was just unhappiness. He knew that Lee-Armour's heart was still on the Bagai plateau, and would remain there, perhaps for years, until some other helpless people won his second and calmer love.

For three long days of travel and camp there was no getting close to the man. His courtesy, his solicitude for his companion's comfort were beyond reproach, but he himself seemed to be writhing in some abyss which he did not dare to have others contemplate, or to contemplate himself. Only once did he show any emotion, and that was when the archdeacon referred to the religion of the Bagai.

'Little and uncomplicated,' said Lee-Armour. 'They believe in a sort of collective soul of the people and another collective soul of the cattle. All the rest they leave to professionals.'

'Their priests?'

'A family group of witch doctors – if one can call them priests.'

'One can,' the archdeacon answered cheerfully. 'Clergy is clergy the whole world over. Provided always that what they serve is the best they can imagine.'

'God knows what they serve,' Lee-Armour exclaimed with sudden bitterness.

'That is just what I meant,' said the archdeacon.

When the journey down to the sea was done and Mark Lee-Armour had gone to his hotel – that, too, was odd when there were a dozen officials in the capital, including the governor himself, who would have been delighted to put him up – the archdeacon unlocked his three-room bungalow, and spent the night awake and upon his knees. Such was his custom and pleasure on return from all the soul-deadening administrative problems of a tour. He looked forward to the long act of worship just as the district commissioner he might so easily have been would have looked forward to his bath and the ice that tinkled in long glasses.

The Archdeacon of the Sultanates had much to occupy the long hours of self-questioning, for he knew what was said of him; that he was discouraging to missionaries, that he was a politician, that he cared more for his few, powerful white rams than his uncounted flock of black sheep. He admitted that the accusations were true, and hoped that the motives ascribed to him were wrong. He was not a snob; but certainly he was convinced that no missionary, if it came to the mere measurement of good works, could surpass the utter devotion and Christian selflessness of such administrators as Lee-Armour, and that it was through them he should work.

He arose refreshed, weary only in body, and at breakfast turned to his timetable of work and engagements – an optimistic schedule which he was never allowed to fulfil. It was so that morning. With the toast and marmalade came a message from the governor, begging him to drop in as soon as possible for a private chat. His imperial self was flattered by so urgent a request, while his other self indulgently smiled at such boyishness.

Governor and archdeacon, as they sat side by side in easy chairs at a significant distance from the official desk, seemed to form the nucleus of a club. They were of the same physical structure, though sedentary life had diverted their bodies, once hard and lean, in two opposite directions. The dark-haired governor was very thin and tall, with an almost professorial stoop; the archdeacon was fairer and smoother and rounder, as if decorously to fill out the apron which he never wore. He had not avoided those worries which contracted the stomach of the governor; he merely placed them in the hands of higher Authority than the Colonial Secretary.

'Toby,' said the governor – for they were on terms of Christian names – 'you travelled down with Mark Lee-Armour. What's wrong with him?'

'I don't know,' the archdeacon answered. 'I wish I did.'

'Then look at that and tell me what you think,' the governor appealed, handing him a letter.

It was an urgent private note from Lee-Armour's successor. It told the governor that the accounts of the Bagai Agricultural Development Fund were twelve hundred pounds short when Lee-Armour handed over, that he had quite calmly admitted the deficit and that he had been unwilling to explain why there were neither vouchers nor receipts. The new commissioner, jealous for the honour of his service, had written unofficially to the governor in the hope that the loss could be adjusted or hushed up before any official cognisance had to be taken of it.

'It can't be *true!*' the governor exclaimed, exasperated by the certainty that it was.

'He was moved unexpectedly?' Archdeacon Toby asked.

'Yes. They've got a high commissionership for him when he gets home, and he only had a few weeks' notice. That's the damnable part of it. It looks as if he has been caught short with his fingers in the kitty, and didn't have time to pay the money back. But I don't believe it. I can't believe it. Lee-Armour of all people!'

The district commissioner's reticence during the journey down was convincingly explained. The archdeacon remembered, too, that when he had watched Lee-Armour saying good-bye to his successor, there had been a tension between them which could not wholly be explained by the inevitable feeling of one that his work would henceforth be in less loving hands, and of the other that he had been given too hard, too individual an example to follow.

'This letter was in the mail he carried down himself?'

'Yes, of course it was,' the governor answered testily.

'That's a pretty good tribute to him from his successor.'

'Tribute? Damn his tribute! What does a chap like Lee-Armour want with tribute from any of us? What on earth am I to do, Toby? And with this thing hanging over us, I've got to make a speech at his farewell banquet tonight. And he and I both knowing that the very next day I may have to refuse him permission to leave!'

'He has always played a very lone hand,' the archdeacon suggested thoughtfully.

'Well, what of it? What else could he do?'

It was true that for eight years Lee-Armour had surrendered his life, his thoughts, his pleasures and the society of his own kind to the welfare of the Bagai. He spoke not only the Bagai language but the private dialects of the family groups, which were almost separate languages in themselves.

They were not everybody's meat, those cattle-owning warriors who drank cow's blood as a staple diet, and shed human – whenever they were reasonably sure they wouldn't be caught. But those who loved them said they were the only free men left in the world. They looked free. They had an engaging habit of painting golden armour on their deep copper skins, and they plastered their hair with cow dung to resemble – though they did not know it – the graceful headdresses of their far-distant Egyptian ancestors. They still lived a little before the dawn of history. Their cattle and their women shared, as necessary companions, this idleness of paradise.

'And I never heard of a missionary making a single worthwhile convert among 'em,' said the governor aggressively, for he was thinking of Lee-Armour and resented all competition with his selfless leadership.

'The Bagai will give us none or all,' said Archdeacon Toby. 'And I may live to see the day when we have all.'

'What? Those bloodthirsty savages?'

'I expect they said the same to Augustine about the Anglo-Saxons,' the archdeacon retorted cheerfully.

Lee-Armour's task had been to begin civilisation, while preserving the flavour of the Golden Age. The Bagai knew very well that if you dug the land and planted seeds you could live on the results. But nothing had ever induced them to try the experiment. They despised agriculture as an occupation proper for the thick-lipped black man whose death at the end of a broad Homeric spear barely counted for graduation from youth to warrior; in fact it didn't count unless carried out with secrecy and craftsmanship, wounds of ingress and egress being checked for neatness by a delegate of the Old Man's committee. That was the tribe whom Lee-Armour must persuade to till the soil.

It had to be done. The Bagai plateau was overstocked with cattle, and there was no more land available. Left to themselves, the warriors would have solved the problem by creating a large empty quarter where their people could wander for the next hundred years; but that solution they knew was finished forever. The only other was the slaughter of unwanted herds – which to them was quite as infamous as to a Christian was Hitler's slaughter of the unfit or undesirable.

The main reason for Lee-Armour's success was his discovery that, although the Bagai would be ashamed to grow food and eat it, there was an absence of tradition either for or against growing food to sell it – a discovery simple enough once stated, but demanding three years of patience in mud huts, of standing to a lion's charge with shield and spear, of visits, interested and respectful, to that hill where the hereditary witch doctors preserved, but seldom, even to the old men, expounded the beliefs and practices of their ancestors.

The result was the much-photographed marketing on the border of the Bagai country. Caravans of government lorries, loaded with sacks of wheat and maize, rolled down from the plateau with chosen warriors sitting on top. The drivers were black, for the Bagai had a truly aristocratic attitude towards engines. A gentleman did not manage such things himself; he enjoyed a chauffeur. Nor did a gentleman haggle over the price. He decided it – and remained for a week, if necessary, casually polishing his spear until it was received. Rather than argue, the Bagai had been known in early days to order drivers and loads back to the highlands. For later harvests, however, Lee-Armour learned to persuade the stern and dung-plastered marketing board that the fair price to ask was exactly that which the government intended to pay.

The crop was rich and regular. As the Bagai were starting from scratch, with no bad habits of their own, they did what the agricultural experts told them. And they had the most amazing luck – beginner's luck, the governor called it. Their experimental estates were not as yet very extensive, but the rains never passed them over in the spring; and if there were storms when the corn was in ear, they broke conveniently on the cattle-lands or beyond the borders of the Bagai.

'What makes me so wild,' said the governor, 'is that I have to bust a saint like Lee-Armour for mislaying twelve hundred pounds. And if he had lost twelve million in that crazy ground-nut project, he'd probably get a knighthood for it. What on earth did he need it for? What made him take such a risk?'

'Better ask him.'

'Of course I'm going to ask him,' the governor fretted. 'And I want you here.'

'Not I,' said Archdeacon Toby.

'You must. I'm not going to expose Lee-Armour even to my own ADC. I won't have anyone official in on this yet. But there it is – I don't know what I'm going to run into. He may be mad. I may find myself compounding a felony. There ought to be a witness.'

'He'll resent it.'

'He won't. He knows as much about this job of mine as I do. He'll realise at once why you are here, and he'll ignore you with the utmost good manners.'

The governor resumed his official chair. The archdeacon effaced himself so far as possible in the hot dusk of the shuttered room. He stayed for Lee-Armour's sake rather than the governor's. That amiable and worried bureaucrat wasn't at his best in any situation of human delicacy, and an audience might stimulate him into his most intelligent behaviour. It did. When the district commissioner came round from the hotel where, puzzling his hospitable colleagues, he had hidden himself, it was as a great, a very great administrator, who had saved the Bagai from despair and his country from a hateful punitive expedition, that the governor greeted him.

Lee-Armour accepted the archdeacon's presence with a tense, charming smile that made the other wince with pity for him. It was a smile which acknowledged the governor's limitations and welcomed the intruder not as a mere necessary evil, but as an obvious first choice. After that he gave his undivided attention to his superior.

Mark Lee-Armour was very much the standard colonial official – sandy, wiry, soldierly, his clean-shaven face burned Arab brown – but the eyes, in a sense, were shifty. They were responsible; they met the governor's own without effort; and, when they looked, they looked straight into the soul; but they would wander off, proudly and impassively, like the eyes of an animal. This uncertainty of glance, giving an impression that there were far more important realities than the present interview, disturbed the archdeacon until he remembered that it was the bored, leonine look of the Bagai warriors themselves.

'Do you feel up to all this tonight, Mark?' the governor asked.

'Yes, sir – if you don't expect me to make much of a speech. I've lost the habit.'

'Just tell us stories about the Bagai,' suggested the governor.

For ten minutes they talked the shop of their devoted trade, occasionally throwing a courteous ball to the archdeacon. Then the governor, his hollow cheeks flushing as they had hardly done since he was at school, came awkwardly to the point.

'Mark, when you handed over were your accounts in

66

order? Balance you know, and all that? Your successor has dropped me a note –'

'He is quite right,' Lee-Armour interrupted.

'But – but didn't you give him any explanation?'

'None. I have none.'

'But what in God's name did you spend it on?'

'I'd rather not say, sir, if you don't mind.'

And again the glance flickered off into the corner of the room as if the smell of the dung fires and the sweet breath of the cattle must somehow be hidden behind the office furniture and could be captured by sudden attention.

'But you – *you*, Mark! Look here, you know you're booked for a high commissionership?'

'I heard it,' he answered without much interest. 'They would take me away for something like that.'

The governor was justifiably annoyed. If ambition were slighted, what was the incentive for a career? Remembering the archdeacon's presence, he pulled himself up. Did men like Lee-Armour – or himself in his first beloved district – ever have to think of promotion in order to give of their best?

'Can you repay the money? Here and now, before the matter goes any further?'

'No, sir.'

'But man, you must have saved something in the last eight years!'

'Nothing. The funds were never quite enough for what I wanted to do. *You* know.'

The governor did. There were always expenses that seemed essential to the man on the spot, and yet could never be justified to any government auditor. A district could be a costly mistress to its lover.

'Wire home for it. I'll risk doing nothing for a couple of days. There must be some way of raising the money.'

'No, sir. No rich relatives,' Lee-Armour replied with a shade of irony. 'Believe me, I've tried everything already.'

'Then you realise there will have to be a full inquiry?'

'I realise to the full that there is a criminal charge hanging over me.'

It was with the coldest inhumanity towards himself that Lee-Armour pronounced the words – words that the governor had tried hard to keep in the back of his mind lest he too should pronounce them. And the man's self-discipline was so absolute that his voice was not even bitter.

'Mark,' begged the governor, shocked into complete unself-consciousness, 'there must be a receipt of some sort. There must be some perfectly honourable explanation. I know you spent that twelve hundred quid on your blasted Bagai.'

'In a way, sir, yes.'

'Then why on earth don't you remember I want to help, and tell me what it was for?'

'Because it would be your duty to take it away from the person I gave it to,' Lee-Armour replied with the directness of a man who, through weeks of agony, had decided how that very question should be answered. 'And that I cannot allow.'

'Bribery?' asked the governor sharply.

It was not unknown for a weak district commissioner to pay out money to possible troublemakers for the preservation of his own peace rather than the King's.

'No, sir. Payment for value received. Received, pressed down and running over.'

Through the half-opened blinds of the long north windows governor and archdeacon watched Lee-Armour walk back across the courtyard to the gates, take the salute of the guard and vanish into the jet-black shadows of the avenue.

Archdeacon Toby, remembering the straightforward accounts of the diocese and his own incompetent arithmetic, said – for the silence had to be broken – that considering all the money which had passed through Lee-Armour's hands for seeds and tools, granaries, lorries and roads it was a marvel to him that twelve hundred pounds could be traced at all.

'You can trace twopence,' the governor snapped.

And so you could. Yet the system was so cumbrous that he had come up before against accounts that wouldn't balance – especially the accounts of queer devoted fish like

Lee-Armour who, with one half of his mind, must be thinking in terms of cattle and tribal custom. The eyes tortured by sun glare, the obsessions, the strain not only of doing justice day by day but of explaining why it was justice – all those could so unbalance a man that he would scream at the inhuman rulings of a ledger.

'We're all worked out beyond sanity,' the governor cried. 'Do you realise what we're doing? Do you realise? It isn't any longer to make the black man white? It's to give him a culture that in two generations shall be more satisfying than our own. And we have all got quite ordinary brains! We aren't gods!'

'There are other Auditors who know it,' said the archdeacon.

'Oh, yes, damn 'em!' answered the governor, missing the overpious comfort in his agitation. 'Some of them *can* be helpful when they like.'

And he reminded the archdeacon of a case like Lee-Armour's where the grim accountants had immediately broken down in smiles at the simplicity of the bookkeeping mistake which had wrecked for months the peace of mind of a first-rate man who imagined he had spent the money when he hadn't.

The archdeacon did not say what he thought. It was Lee-Armour's pride which bothered him, his awareness that he was wrecking his career for the sake of the Bagai. There had been no bookkeeping mistake. Lee-Armour was a man to take routine accounting in his stride. And even if there had been a mistake, his successor, coming straight from leave with a fresh mind, would have spotted it. However, there was no point in depriving the governor of the grain of comfort he had found for himself.

'I'm sure that for tonight, at any rate,' said Archdeacon Toby, 'we should assume this is a case where the accountants would only smile.'

The farewell dinner was in the hotel garden. The dark was hot as day but an illusion of coolness was created by the plashing of a fountain, the smell of wet earth and night-flowering shrubs, the ice in the wine-buckets, the white uniforms of servants; and by the guests who numbered themselves among Lee-Armour's friends but should more truly have been called acquaintances. His intimate friends were scattered among the provinces that bordered the Bagai country – one of them to perhaps every fifty thousand square miles.

For Lee-Armour's sake the archdeacon was glad; it would be easier for him to keep up pretences in the presence of people who were either attaching themselves to his legend, or eagerly following the star that was inevitably going to rise to the zenith of the Colonial Office. Archdeacon Toby, in the intervals of talking archidiaconally to the ardent churchwomen placed to right and left of him, watched the group at the head of the horseshoe table. Lee-Armour, sitting between the wives of governor and chief justice, was impassive, playing with perfect good manners the easy part of a strong, silent man. The governor, too, seemed to be acting without effort. Such a party was, of course, routine for him once it had begun, once he had fairly accustomed himself to entertaining and praising the man whom, the very next day, he must order to remain in the colony while his accounts were investigated. He had presided over so much false and real geniality that when he rose to speak the right words came to him. Indeed, it was the warmest little after-dinner speech that Archdeacon Toby had ever heard the governor deliver – the result, no doubt, of a deliberate effort not to be cold. In a social crisis, thought the archdeacon, world, flesh and devil certainly had their uses.

Mark Lee-Armour rose to reply. Platitudes, interesting platitudes (what a governor he would make!) until suddenly a moving sincerity quickened his voice. The archdeacon knew that he was listening to his swan-song, to words that Lee-Armour intended to be remembered after the truth came out.

'Honour. That, I think, is the common bond. It doesn't matter how primitive a people are; they still have some conception of honour. I remember – you all have these memories – one of my Bagai warriors. He killed an Arab trader. I gave him five years. That's the death sentence of course; they don't last in prison more than one. He took it like a man. You see, to his way of thinking, he had done the honourable thing. He told me so. 'And this sentence,' I answered, 'is for the honour of my King.' 'Then, my lord,' he said, in that casual tone of an eighteenth-century aristocrat they can put on, 'we both suffer for the welfare of my people, for both are ants crushed between the Bagai and your King." '

Lee-Armour sat down amid an uproarious rattle of applause. Nobody except archdeacon and governor perceived any special point in the story, but it was enough that Lee-Armour had told it and that the party was going well.

The women had seen to it that there was dancing after the dinner. Groups splitting up between the hotel bar, the dance floor and the gardens, allowed Archdeacon Toby to withdraw unnoticed. He had no intention of going home, for he knew very well where his duty lay, and hoped that Providence would give him an opportunity to perform it.

Lurking in the shadows – meditating, he preferred to call it – he kept a careful eye upon the garden bar where Lee-Armour drifted along the edge of a little crowd, avoiding confinement in its centre. He was certain that the man longed to be alone, and that his mood would now be of deep melancholy brought on by the moderate drinking which, as guest of honour, he hadn't been able to evade. Lee-Armour would not endure much longer the bitter irony of his fare-well dinner; on the other hand he would not yet retire – since that would be churlish – to his hotel bedroom.

Archdeacon Toby told himself that he had no intention of thrusting his society upon private loneliness nor – certainly not! – of spying upon it. Yet, when he saw Lee-Armour slip away from the bar and vanish into the culti-vated jungle of tropical shrubs which bordered the garden, he followed. Beyond the garden, on the edge of the river flats, the shadow of Lee-Armour moved among the moon shadows of a line of silent palms which striped the sand. And then indeed was Archdeacon Toby guilty of all that hypocrisy with which the missionaries reproached him. With his hands behind his back and an air of pious abstraction he too began to pace among the palms.

He had already passed the lonely figure and wished it good-night when he pretended to recognise who it was.

'I am so very sorry about this morning,' he said. 'I shouldn't have been there.'

'I was glad it was you,' Lee-Armour answered frankly. 'I suppose H. E. had to have somebody, and it was decent of him not to call in anyone official as yet.'

'He's inclined to think now that you made a mistake in the accounts,' said the archdeacon.

Lee-Armour's low voice was angry – a man who was never afraid to face facts exasperated by the proneness of his opposite type to self-deception.

'Good Lord, didn't I make it clear? Didn't I make it clear that I never did anything more deliberate in my life?'

'You made it crystal clear.'

'Good Lord, it was a deliberate payment when I knew that I was going! The best I could do for my people. The Bagai must *not* despair. I won't have police and shooting after I've gone.'

'I don't want to intrude,' said the archdeacon, 'but if it would do you any good to tell a neutral . . .'

'It would do me good. In all this nonsense –' he waved a hand towards the distant lights and the unfamiliar beat of drums in a sentimental waltz '– I'm wondering if I'm mad, if I have or haven't gone native. Do you people still observe the seal of confession?'

'Doubtfully,' answered the archdeacon, 'like so much. Perhaps it would be more honest if at this hour and place I offered you my word of honour.'

'Look here – I gave that money to a witch doctor. I don't know what he serves. I doubt if he knows himself. But it is not *our* God.'

'There is no other,' Archdeacon Toby replied. 'The First Commandment is, for our days, rather oddly worded. "Thou shalt have none other gods" should be, "There are no other gods". What did you want God to do for the witch doctor?'

'To make the rain fall when it was needed. To prevent the rain falling when it was not.'

'Twelve hundred pounds seems a lot,' the archdeacon heard himself saying, as he tried to order his thoughts into an act of divine worship and human understanding.

'No. The bargain was for as long as he should live. He was to do nothing else. And he has expenses, and no cattle like the rest of them.'

'He can do it?'

'He always has in the past. Look at the statistics.'

'That was what they called beginner's luck?'

'Yes. Luck. A little tilting of the balances. I don't know how they do it. But it's no good telling me – or most of us out here – that they can't.'

'If I told you that they couldn't, I should be unworthy of priesthood,' the archdeacon answered gently, knowing himself to be on the solid ground of theology.

'They have powers we have not got?'

'We have all the powers that they have. But to use them – that demands, I fear, a simplicity which only our saints can attain.'

To him, as a deeply read churchman, every religion – of the past or of primitive present – had its value in so far as it foreshadowed the mysteries of the Faith. He believed with all his heart that those truths which man had feebly tried to utter through myth and magic were finally formulated by God in Christianity. Thus the prayers of the Church for rain and for delivery from storm and tempest were the divinely established ritual, but not the only possible ritual.

'I thought you would be the last person to approve,' said Lee-Armour wonderingly.

'I did not say I approved,' the archdeacon replied. 'Only that I believed. Dear son, I have been in Africa long enough to know that sometimes, very rarely, men are given control over rain and over animals. I myself am so made that I have never doubted God shut the mouths of the lions for Daniel in the den. Nevertheless one's faith is firmer when one has seen – as I have seen – the tribal priest shut the mouths of the crocodiles at the bathing pool.'

'Yes,' said Lee-Armour, 'I've heard of that. It's quite safe to swim when he has given the word.'

'I found it so.'

'Then you at least will understand that I am paying a small price for my Bagai.'

'The price was twelve hundred pounds,' Archdeacon Toby answered, smiling. 'Not a big cheque for me to draw, I think, for rain and peace. And for my own peace, too. Shall we go back to the hotel? I want to tell the governor that there has been a mistake, a very subtle mistake, and that the money has now been debited to the right account.'

Exiles

Pain, slight but continuous, limited any excited curiosity about the English passing through his life, pink ghosts who looked through him and flowed onwards unseeing. Before he left Africa he had been told that among the young he would find no colour prejudice, but that he must expect little more than politeness from their fathers. Both, to start with, would be neutral. He had found the official warning pretty true until his accident.

In the hospital there had been no such neutrality, nothing but sympathy and undisturbed kindliness. All of them understood how desolate an experience it was to be maimed by a careless driver in so foreign a country. He had been content to trust the hypnotic confidence of surgeons until they returned him to normal life, telling him to come back once a week for examination. They even cared how much money he had and how he would live. That astonished him. The overcrowded hospitals of his own country inevitably threw their patients out as soon as possible and told them to get on with their business as best they could.

He was all right. He had enough money – after spending so little for so long – to live at the hotel in the market town where the ambulance had taken him. He would have preferred London and less loneliness, but shrank from being mauled once a week by strange doctors with whom he had no bond. That was natural enough. Yet the indifference of provincial life depressed him. There was no one to talk to – about pain or kindness or Africa or anything else.

Not that he was ever ignored. He was a young curiosity like the talking mynah hopping about its cage behind the cashier's desk. His waiter, the hotel staff, the receptionist were punctilious in remarking that it was a nice day or

75

asking how his leg was. When it rained, somebody always said: 'I expect you wish you were back in Africa.' He did, but not for the reason they thought. The rain revived his memories of pouring, tropical warmth. It was not rain which he hated, but the lack of any sun warm enough to dry.

After leaving his solitary table in the dining-room he sat in a corner of the lounge where his face faded into the dark wallpaper behind. He felt an instinctive sense of security as if he were a child watching inexplicable strangers from the embracing roots of a tree. But he did not want security. He had enough of it.

He asked himself what he did want. The answer was immediate. Freedom from pain and a girl – though that could lead to unthinkable humiliation since as yet there had been little sign of returning virility. Perhaps above all he wanted someone with whom to laugh noisily and happily. Little hope of that. Talk was not important to these English. Also they could not always understand what he said unless he spoke slowly. It was not in his nature to speak slowly. Words should tumble like water in and out of the shade and over the shallows of laughter.

Outside, in the street, an unreal procession passed the window. Mostly they were young and gay. They were not so lively as his own people, but at least they gave the impression of being glad to be together, of not requiring any definite action or objective before they could appear alive. Large men, their backsides moulded to the seats of cars, passed across his front on their way from the bar to the Gents Lavatory. That was the only effect on them of alcohol. Then two middle-aged women in pink hats entered his lonely half of the lounge, saw him, started and changed their minds about sitting down. Did they think he was likely to dance and shout, or to show indecent interest in their clumsy bodies?

An old man came into the lounge from the twilight of the street. Perhaps not so old. It was hard to tell with some of these up-country Englishmen. They remained slim instead of acquiring the weight and dignity of age, and their blood-shot eyes had still some sparkle of youth. In London he had seen few such men; in this market town there were more. That was to be expected. The retired clerks in the villages of his own land did not look so spirited as the old farmers.

His casual glance of inspection was answered and held, while the other at once and eagerly crossed the room.

'May I sit down?' he asked.

Too gentle a request and strange. It was for the young to ask the old if they might sit down.

'Ah, but we are not in your country,' said the grey-haired stranger, smiling as if he were able to read thoughts.

'I am not a West Indian.'

He was weary of being taken for a West Indian, but a little startled by the abruptness of his own reply. He assured himself that it was not due to shame because his own warlike people had captured and sold slaves; it was simply that a difference of manners existed between West Indian and African, perhaps resembling that between American and European. One gave little importance to dignity and the other gave too much.

'I know you are not. I recognised the tribal mark.'

'You have been in my country?' he asked.

'I was a district commissioner for twenty years.'

That was difficult. He had been brought up on so many stories of District Commissioners – of their justice, their humanity, their occasional uncomprehending cruelty. His grandfather grumbled that the country had been better off under the British. His father said neither better nor worse, but that now they had freedom; now they were men. For himself the life before independence was hazy and hard to explain. Governors, district commissioners and the rest of them were a mystery of the past. They had no right on their side, so they ought to have been hated. Yet they had not been hated.

'Did you like my people?'

'I loved them. I always shall. How did you hurt your leg?'

'A car hit me. I have been in hospital.'

'Here?'

The tone of voice suggested that it was so rustic a hospital or perhaps so unlikely a town.

77

'All of them looked after me. I have never known such kindness.'

'Yes, they would,' he agreed. 'The surgeons are first-rate and have time for the personal touch as well. I meant that in London you would not feel so far from home.'

The old man broke into a Swahili which was purer and more fluent than his own, the words singing like rain on burned, eroded ground. He did not want to reply, but the grey evening of a grey town was unsuited to the language which this former giver of law spoke with such commanding joy. Yet, after all, it was irresistible. The words began to tumble out of him – of his home, his parents and the cattle, of the customs of England, of his examinations passed and his hope of a place in a university.

'And somebody is keeping the eye of a father on you?'

He lied cheerfully that somebody was, for it was not good to be thought without powerful friends. But men are busy.

'Are you married?' he asked this elder. 'Have you many children?'

'No, I never married. There was no time.'

It seemed curious that a boss politician who had enjoyed such opportunities for making money should not now be comforted by sons and grandsons.

'At least you are now at home,' he said. 'And that is good, very good.'

'At home, yes. But when a man has given his life, it stays where he gave it. I do not see what they see.' He opened his yellow hand towards two prosperous, pink salesmen exchanging heavily printed cards as they left the bar. 'I do not feel what they feel. That is why I could not pass one of my people without seeing if he was in need.'

He sounded like a missionary with this talk of love and *his* people. That could never have been the way of district commissioners. They had been great men, too proud to seek companionship from wounded students. They did not, he was sure, ask if they might sit down.

It was his hour for the special, weekly visit to the hospital. He struggled to his feet, the bright steel supports faintly clinking between knee and ankle.

'I will drive you there and wait for you.'

'I am a man,' he answered resentfully. 'I will go out alone.'

Red Carpet Treatment

To a tired American who, on her second day in England, had just missed her train back to London and had two hours to wait for another, it had looked all that a small hotel ought to be – green and white, built in the days before Stanborough had become an industrial town, with a front door opening upon a quiet courtyard flanked by eighteenth-century houses.

Inside, however, it was utterly without welcome. Two old ladies were knitting on a sofa. A retired military man – at a guess – was asleep in front of an inadequate electric fire. A party of three men in a corner had busy glasses and ash-trays in front of them, but seemed affected by the general hush.

She just sat. Nobody paid any attention to her. It was nearly as cold as the railroad junction. After a while the uncompromising back of the manageress was to be seen behind the glass of the combined bar and office at the back of the lounge.

'Three doubles, please!'

The manageress carried a tray of whiskies over to the three men. She showed exemplary patience at the disturbance.

'Can I have some dinner?' Janet asked as she passed.

'I am sorry, dinner is finished.'

'A sandwich will do.'

'I am sorry, we do not serve food in the lounge to non-residents.'

The creature vanished among its account books and bottles. Janet felt that the universe had run down and time had ceased. The two old ladies tottered off to bed. The major woke himself up with a complicated snore, looked anxiously round the lounge and marched out.

The three men were left, enjoying themselves decorously over drinks. Their quietness annoyed her. If they couldn't be more lively after those large doses of alcohol, when could they be? They were tall, dressed in good tweeds and in their thirties. All looked exasperatingly alike, though she had to admit that they weren't. One was clean-shaven; one had a dark moustache; and the third a fair moustache.

They had looked up and smiled at her encounter with that intolerable woman, but Janet had not responded. A minute later she decided that the smiles were sympathetic, but it was too late. They ignored her politely – all except fair moustache of whose eyes she was occasionally aware.

Twenty interminable minutes passed. An unshaven porter in dirty shirt and green baize apron put his head through the bar hatch and said:

'Time, gentlemen, please!'

Dark moustache looked at his watch.

'Nonsense – it's not half past ten yet! And this lady has been waiting half an hour to be served.'

'The missus says it's time,' replied the porter.

He crashed down the bar hatch with the finality of a guillotine and disappeared.

Janet got up, thankful that the spell which had condemned her to see and not be seen was broken. The three men also rose.

'Madam,' said fair moustache, 'I can only hope that you have graced this country long enough to know that all our hotels are not like this.'

'I guess there are hellholes everywhere,' Janet replied a little too emphatically, and then smiled.

They stood before her with such an air of concern and apology. They swayed very gently like benevolent eleph-ants, but there was nothing else in speech or manner to suggest that the order of 'three doubles' had been repeated for most of the evening.

'Mike,' asked clean-shaven, 'the red carpet?'

'Indubi-dubitably, Jim,' answered Mike-fair-moustache.

'The lady has been humiliated, and she shall leave this hellhole, as she so rightly described it, with befitting dignity.'

Forty feet of bright crimson carpet ran from the front door across the lounge, past the bar hatch and down a passage. Jim and Mike walked straight out of the door with the leading edge. Dark moustache reluctantly followed with the rear end as if he were holding up a bride's train. They spread the carpet down the steps and across the courtyard.

Their attitudes respectfully suggested Sir Walter Raleigh and his cloak. She hesitated. But there was no other way of leaving the hotel. She walked the length of the carpet disapprovingly, then giggled and swept the three a graceful curtsey.

The front door slammed.

'Glad to get rid of us even if it costs 'em a carpet, Noll,' said the clean-shaven Jim.

'You and Mike. . . .' began Noll-dark-moustache severely.

He was interrupted by an inviting hiss from the level of the pavement. The hoarse whisper of that unspeakable porter came from a grating under the steps.

'Neat! Very neat! I ain't seen nothink, see? I was down 'ere with the furnace, see? You got two minutes before she comes back to check the bar takin's. We could nick 'alf the pub if you and me gets together. Ask for Len at Bob's Pull-in Café.'

'This,' said Mike, staring at the shut door, 'comes under the head of Things-which-were-funny-at-the-time.'

'But we can't run away like a bunch of juvenile delinquents,' Noll protested. 'Ring the bell and put it back!'

'Ring, hell! How long is it going to take that manageress to see a joke? And with Len swearing blind that he stopped us getting away with it, which he would . . .'

'JP accused of stealing carpet,' said Noll in a voice which quoted headlines.

'What's a JP?' Janet asked.

'I am – and it's what you call a judge.'

'Roll it up and leave it in the backyard,' Mike proposed decisively.

Between the silent houses which lined the court was a narrow passage. The three rolled up the carpet with one hearty shove, carried it through the alley and put it in the back of a parked station-wagon.

'Hop in!' Mike invited. 'You're too conspicuous.'

'I don't see how, or that it matters.'

'Hair auburn. Complexion pale. Dressed in grey-green suit. Height five foot seven. Build slight. Speaks with American accent, possibly assumed. Suspected alias, Carpet Kate.'

Janet, sounding to herself too impeccably formal, replied that her name was Janet Morland and that she was catching the 11.05 back to London.

'You shall. Noll, we must go round two corners and think this out.'

'Now, I'd better introduce your fellow criminals,' said Noll as the car rolled away. 'I am Oliver Cromwell. Can't help it. I really am. Descended from the same family. This is Jim Blaize, Clerk to the Justices. I have warned him before not to nick carpets in bars where they aren't used to him. And this party with the ginger moustache is Michael Lanchester. He is a wicked squire and farms. We're all from the next county and nobody knows us here in Stanborough – or I'd go straight to the police station and fix this silly business.'

'It wouldn't be easy to keep it quiet even at home,' Mike Lanchester remarked.

'It would,' said Jim. 'I've told that local reporter of ours that if he doesn't leave the pair of us out of his news it's going to be justifiable homicide when I sit on his body.'

Janet froze. She was in a strange country and she had only been there thirty-six hours. She had always heard that English country gentry were the most correct of human beings with the possible exception of Chinese mandarins. Still, homicide . . .

'I forgot to mention that Jim is also the Coroner,' said Oliver Cromwell.

At the back of the hotel was a high blank wall with one small door in it. On the opposite side of the street were no houses, only locked garages, more walls and a builder's yard. Janet was relieved. Under such favourable circumstances even three lunatics could return a carpet.

'All we have to do,' said Noll, 'is to stand on the roof of Mike's car, pass the carpet up to a chap on the wall and pitch it over. I'll just go up and see where it will fall.'

He climbed from the car onto the coping of the wall.

'There's a lean-to shed on this side,' he reported. 'If we roll the carpet down the slates it will land right in front of the hotel's back door. The old girl can't miss it.'

He hunched himself along the wall, and stood up to get a better view of a lit window.

'She has telephoned the cops already,' he whispered. 'I can see 'em in there. Smart police force in Stanborough! It's a curious thing,' he added confidingly to Janet, 'I've no head for heights and I'd never have dared to stand on this wall in daylight. Yet here I am at night steady as a rock with absolute . . .'

The rending crash was succeeded by a trickle of falling slates and an instant's silence. Then action broke out all along the front. A whistle blew. Two doors slammed in the hotel. There was a splintering explosion as Noll showed he was still alive by knocking out some window which he couldn't open. Mike Lanchester started the car. The justice of the peace shot out of the door in the wall covered with cobwebs and plaster.

'Damn it, I went through the roof!' he said.

A second later they were cruising innocently through the well-lit streets.

'The next thing is to put Miss Morland on her train,' Mike said firmly, 'before she has to send for her consul to bail her out.'

He drove very carefully down a long street of little red-brick houses until the lights of the station were a hundred yards ahead.

'Stop!' Janet ordered, and nearly went through the windscreen.

'Sorry! I thought you saw a bicyclist without a rear light.'

'I just remembered that I told the hotel female I was waiting for a train,' she explained.

'Oh, the police won't believe that!' said Jim Blaize. 'They'll think it was your cover story.'

'One never knows what they will or won't believe,' Noll warned, gloomily fishing for bits of slate inside his shirt. 'When they stopped the car with all Mike's silver from the manor in it, they waved him on again because he said his mother was ill.'

'I'll go with her,' said Mike, taking immediate charge.

Janet liked the proprietary air with which he accompanied her to the station as if he were seeing off a guest.

'This sort of thing always happens as soon as one arrives in a foreign country or not at all,' he said. 'I wish we could have met more formally.'

She responded at once.

'I'd never forgive you if you didn't write to me care of the consulate and tell me what happened.'

'You'll probably see it in tomorrow's evening paper anyway. Well, here we are!'

They entered the booking hall. By the ticket collector's box, stolidly examining the passengers for London, were two constables.

'Turn round quietly as if we had just been checking the timetables and walk straight back to the car!' Mike whispered. 'They haven't spotted us yet.'

All went well while they crossed the station courtyard. Then they heard a shout of 'Hey!'

'Don't look round! Pretend it can't possibly be meant for us!'

But it was. Janet gave a hitch to her pencil skirt and ran. The car was already turned and the door open. They beat the constables to it by three seconds.

'That is the end,' Mike Lanchester said as they shot off into a network of obscure streets. 'Even if we get clear they can trace the car to me.'

Jim remarked cheerfully that they had dealt with the evidence while the two were away. A piece of sacking hanging out from the boot had got tied round the rear numberplate, and Noll had decorated the front with engine oil.

'But it's all very well,' Noll said. 'I'm going to surrender and explain as best I can. We can't get clear without some tricky driving and we are none of us sober enough. Slow and cautious, yes. Fast, no. I gave a bloke three months last week for thinking he could drive because he could still talk.'

Janet approved. If they had to stand in the dock while their story was telephoned through to eager sub-editors it was just too bad, but they deserved it. Still, it did seem specially hard on Mike who wasn't a judge or a coroner or anything else. And why specially, she asked herself. Oh, well . . .

'I shall drive,' she said. 'I've been in rallies, and I've got an international driving licence.'

'I don't think it's good here unless you register it. But that,' Noll added hopefully, 'is a minor crime.'

'Where to?' she insisted.

'The first cop who will believe us. And he's thirty miles away. And we daren't take any of the main routes out of town.'

'It looks as if we could get on to the Gloucester road by going down past the gas-works and along a track,' said the coroner, studying the map.

To judge by the protests from the other two, Jim Blaize was famous for optimistic short cuts. But they could suggest nothing better.

'To the gas-works, Kate, if I can find 'em,' Mike said. 'And we drive on the left of the road.'

The gas-works were complicated by the presence of a brewery and a flour mill. All the lanes between them ended at gates or loading bays.

'I think this must be right,' said Jim Blaize at last, pointing to a narrow cinder track across a marshy, derelict field.

Noll pointed out that if it was wrong they could never turn round.

'We could always set fire to Mike's car and walk.'

'But what about the carpet?' Noll asked.

'I'd forgotten the carpet.'

Janet drove slowly ahead, the wheels crunching over cinders. Water seemed to be multiplying on all sides. They came to a barrier of iron railings with a gate only half shut.

'Bit of luck!' Jim exclaimed, getting out to open it. 'If there's a gate at the other end, we're away!'

As she passed through, the headlights shone on a maze of tanks and ponds connected by batteries of pipes. It was evidently the town waterworks or sewage farm. Probably both, she reflected bad-temperedly. And did they let off first offenders in this country or just allow them to use lipstick after the first month inside?

Mike seemed instinctively to realise her sudden panic.

'You're a lovely driver,' he said. 'This track seems to have been made for two wheelbarrows to pass in safety.'

'Wheelbarrows don't skid,' Janet answered, hastily correcting another where the cinders had worn to dust and solidified the mud.

The gate at the far end was chained and padlocked. There was no passing it without a hacksaw and no room to turn; but the track, with a ditch on both sides, curved round to follow the fence. It seemed to be a ringroad circling the plant.

At the next corner the ditches disappeared and the navigable area opened out, sloping up to a sludge tank on the left and down to level grass on the right. It suggested the banking on a miniature race track.

Janet slightly accelerated round the bend and was instantly out of control. She stopped with one rear wheel balanced uncertainly on the edge of the tank.

'Skating rink,' said Mike Lanchester, getting out to inspect the surface. 'The tank has been leaking, and that nice, tempting surface is two inches of mud over smooth stone. The grass is all right if you take it steady.'

The three men got out and bounced the rear end of the car down the slope.

The ringroad took them back again to the entrance. Just as they were about to pass through and return to the gas-works a purposeful car entered the track at the town end. It could only be the police.

'Had to expect it with our lights wandering about the low ground like a lot of blasted pixies!' Noll groaned. 'Now you, dear Carpet Kate, run like hell, climb the fence, find a respectable-looking driver on the Gloucester road and vanish! We shall deny all knowledge of you.'

Janet prepared to do so. She wasn't going to be arrested, probably brutally, in a sewage farm just for mixing with coroners and squires. Didn't they run the damned police anyway? And if they thought of their public positions instead of behaving like a lot of port-soaked bucks . . . but that was mean. And it was narrow-minded to be more afraid of English gaols than American. She was not going to desert them. And with the decision came inspiration.

'Noll, I like to think this is a waterworks,' she said. 'But whatever it is we leave it in company. Just you remember your great ancestor because the Lord has delivered them into our hands or whatever it wasn't he said.'

As the car came bounding through the gate she fled away in front. The police could certainly drive, even on an eight-foot wide cinder track, but she had been over it before and they had not. At the padlocked gate she hesitated an instant as if to confirm that it was shut, and then shot off by the ringroad with the police car ten yards behind.

On the curve where the track widened Janet took the grass. The police, seeing a chance to pass and get in front, swung round the top of the banking. There was a black fountain of sludge as they skidded slap over the edge into the tank.

A roar of delight went up from the three men. They waved out of the windows. Janet, grinning happily to herself, kept on course for the open gate and the gas-works.

'Stop!' the coroner ordered. 'Carpet Kate, we are going to kiss you.'

They did. She noticed that Mike Lanchester was a little shy about it. It might be that he was the only one who really wanted to.

'How ever did you think of it?' Noll asked.

'Just uninhibited,' Janet replied. 'I guess I haven't your British respect for the police.'

'Well, it's total war now. We'll have the whole county out after us. Jim, can they use their radio with the car on its side and the antenna under – er – water?'

'Not for some minutes anyway.'

'There's only one safe place in this town where we are never interrupted,' said Mike. 'Behind that damned hotel! And it's the last place they're going to look for us.'

They reached the back alley without passing a cop, switched off the lights and lit cigarettes. Noll produced a bottle of whisky.

'Medical stores,' he said. 'Badly needed.'

'A stiff one for Carpet Kate,' Mike prescribed, 'and none for me. I'm cold sober now and I'll take over. There's likely to be a long, hard chase, and we don't want her involved.'

Janet accepted her stiff one, for she felt all loose muscles beginning to tremble with the reaction. Her past moments of panic seemed silly. Of course they could have got her out of any serious trouble. But now, as Noll had said, it was total war. Whatever the police chose to swear after that sludge tank, she couldn't blame them. She was thankful to hand over responsibility for her future to Mike.

He wrapped Janet up in a rug and earnestly discussed with her the different traffic laws of England and the State of New York. The coroner and Noll quite unconsciously lowered the level of the bottle and at intervals patrolled the two ends of the street.

'They must think we have left town by now,' said Jim after an hour.

'If we keep to the side roads we should be all right,' Noll agreed. 'So we'll just return the carpet and go.'

There was a general protest at Noll's exaggerated sense of duty.

'Nonsense!' he said. 'And it would be much safer than putting on a false beard and sending the thing back by rail. They forgot to lock the door in the wall here.'

It was true. The massive cylinder of carpet was cautiously carried into the yard and dropped.

'Better put it under cover,' Noll advised. 'It has rained every night since the end of April.'

There was no cover handy. The shed through which Oliver Cromwell, JP, had exploded was surrounded by too much debris for quiet movement. Jim tried the handle of the hotel's back door. That too had been forgotten in the excitement.

'Why not lay it back in the lounge exactly as we found it?' he suggested. 'That will fox the old girl. She'll think she dreamed it all.'

To Janet's horror Mike Lanchester's fancy also seemed to be tickled by the idea – but on condition that he himself went inside first to report whether the scheme was sane and practical.

He was back within a minute.

'No snags,' he said. 'Two steps up and we're in the passage leading to the lounge. Unroll from this end, and the job's done!'

There was a soft thud as they negotiated the steps. Janet held her breath. No sound came from the sleeping hotel. But now the carpet, compressed by an evening of idle travel, took command. The forty feet of it were impatient to unroll. As soon as it had been deposited at the back of the passage and encouraged with a gentle push it gathered speed, making a bee-line for the lounge and the front door.

The width filled the passage so that it was impossible to get in front and stop it. All right if it continued straight, disastrous if it didn't. Knick-knacks and spindly tables were all over the place. Jim Blaize hurdled the roll, tripped as it flicked him across the back of the knees, but still managed to fall with the silence of long practice in juvenile delinquency.

The last yard of carpet slapped into position opposite the front door. Mike patted down a wrinkle in the middle and stepped back to admire their joint handiwork. A heavy wrought-iron standard lamp immediately behind him tottered, avoided his grasp and crashed through the glass partition of the bar.

Upstairs someone screamed. Lights in the lounge suddenly blazed. As the four shot out of the back door and

90

across the yard a large piece of crockery hurled from an upstairs window burst on the stone paving. The car leaped out of the alley and then rolled more sedately through back streets to avoid suspicion.

'This is the end,' Noll declared. 'Can anyone think of any believable explanation when we're accused of coming back to pinch liquor from the bar?'

'If you had only been drinking, Mike, you'd have been more careful,' said Jim reproachfully.

Janet silently agreed and realised that she had accepted English logic. She knew exactly what Jim meant.

'Well, we're all right for the present,' Noll said as soon as they were clear of houses and heading north along by-roads.

'Don't count on it!' Mike muttered, driving in a fury of concentration. 'We passed a cop on the beat. He was too late for action but he recognised the car. We'll double back south here and make for home.'

Janet dozed, her eyes tired by the continual flicking past of white hawthorn blossom in the hedgerows. At intervals they stopped to consult map and sign-posts. Then Mike seemed to be in his own country and was twisting from village to village with confidence.

'Once across the main road, and we're safe,' he said. 'Oh, my God!'

At the junction, tucked away under trees, was a black police car. By the time he had roared two hundred yards down the main road and screeched right into a lane which looked as if it led nowhere the police were in hot pursuit.

Hidden by two corners he shot into a farmyard and round the back of a barn. The police car went straight on. Janet waited for the noise to die away. It did not. The car was turning.

'Can't shake 'em off!' Mike cursed. 'When they don't see my lights they know I've gone to earth. And I daren't drive without till we have a reasonable lead.'

He raced back to the main road, trying sheer speed in the hope of getting away while the police were still in the lane, but there was no wood or valley to hide the gleam of the headlights.

A car ahead laid a false trail for them. Mike pulled into a side turning and watched the police shoot past.

'That gives us a minute till they find out it isn't us,' he said. 'Noll, have you fished up as far as Norton Bridge?'

'Lots of times. I don't suppose they'll ever allow me on their water again after this.'

'What's the bottom like?'

'Gravel. Why?'

'You'll see.'

He turned and tore back up the main road. But the police car was deadly fast, and its lights were already on their tail when he swung left and put on a brilliant burst of speed over tight, continual curves.

Janet saw the little river ahead and thought he had gone crazy. He switched out his lights and, instead of crossing the bridge, bumped down an old paved track to the side of it. He entered the water and turned downstream, pushing a two-foot wave in front of him. Under the bridge he stopped. The police roared over, and on out of sight and hearing.

'I thought it might work if the bottom was hard,' he said. 'No one would notice the track down to the old ford unless he knew it was there. I'll have that drink now, Noll, if there's any left.'

Janet's violent introduction to the eccentricities of England was succeeded by a sleepy delight as the May dawn slowly made love to her. It was heaven to sit in a boat – she couldn't always be remembering it was a station-wagon – conscious of this improbable and attractive Mike Lanchester while the clear stream rippled past and the solid green of the banks, dense and mysterious as jungle, was framed by the arch of the bridge. An otter arrowed upstream and investigated with nose and whiskers the curious obstruction in its fishing ground.

Just before sunrise the three men got out, cleaned the number plates and washed the car to a state of sturdy innocence.

'Now then,' said Mike, 'will she start?'

She did. The coroner went up to the bridge to signal if any traffic came in sight. The justice of the peace stood by the bonnet ready to heave. The squire reversed back to the ford and up onto the road.

'We had better split up now in case of accidents,' Mike proposed. 'You and Jim can easily walk home from here.'

'It's a bit far for Miss Morland,' Noll replied, suddenly becoming formal on the edge of his own country.

'She's coming back to the manor with me. It's obvious that she must take her bath and breakfast with the only bachelor. Both your wives are angels of understanding, but turning up for breakfast with an incoherent story and a devastatingly attractive American . . .'

'He's right,' said Janet hastily. 'I mean – about the explaining.'

'Well, I can leave you in Mike's hands with absolute confidence,' Noll assured her.

Janet replied that of course he could, and rebuked herself for a slight sense of disappointment.

'Now, we'll fix her up so that she doesn't answer the police description. A scarf right over the hair. Jim's duffle coat. And there you are! Anyone would assume that her hair was dark. She has the innocent little madonna face which goes with it. Bring her over to lunch, Mike, and we'll celebrate!'

The two said goodbye and strolled off up the road.

'Is it far to the manor?' Janet asked.

'About five miles. But I'm going round through the lanes. We still don't want to answer questions.'

She could see by the villages and their church towers, which were always off to the right or left, that he was skilfully avoiding early risers. At last they emerged from desolate little roads, where gates had to be opened and shut, on to a straight highway.

'Now,' he said, 'two minutes of this and we're home!'

The car was just gathering speed when a constable leapt out of the hedge ahead and stationed himself bravely and majestically in the middle of the road with upraised hand.

'Oh, it's you, sir!' he said, disappointed. 'Thought I'd got 'em!'

'Who did you think it was, Tompkins?' Mike asked. 'What's the trouble?'

'Nasty business up in Stanborough last night, sir. Police from both counties on the job. They chased a car of the same make as yours and lost it around Norton Bridge.'

'Any description?'

'Not much good. Three well-dressed men and a woman –' he consulted his notes '– American, good-looking, slim build, 'air red . . .'

'Sounds attractive,' Mike interrupted. 'I'm just giving Miss Morland a lift back from London. Rather a late theatre party, I'm afraid.'

'It *was* from London, if you don't mind my asking? She didn't stop you and beg a lift and you, bein' always good-'arted, gave it?'

'Good Lord, no! Miss Morland is an old friend of the family.'

The constable in spite of his air of deference had his eyes too firmly fixed on Janet. She had to say something. She drew a deep breath and produced a magnificent English accent.

'Oh, darling!' she exclaimed to Mike with a bored laugh. 'How really too absurd!'

'Well, good morning, sir,' said the constable. 'Time we both 'ad our breakfast!'

He recovered his bicycle from the hedge and rode away.

'Splendid!' Mike told her. 'Splendid! But the 'darling' was altogether too stagey. We must practise that. Now look me straight in the eyes and say it again!'

The Singular Story of Mr Hackafree

It was only Bill Hackafree who actually saw him. Bill was all alone in his cottage on a Monday night in early February and a gale storming up from the west with a touch of north in it when he heard someone clear his throat, as much as to excuse himself for demanding attention, and noticed a stranger leaning up against the dresser with one hand in his coat pocket and the other fingering his tie. In spite of the weather he was wearing dark glasses and a red silk shirt with his initials on it like one of the summer visitors.

'Shut the door,' said Bill Hackafree, 'and stop that bloody draught!'

'I never opened it,' the stranger said.

'Ah, that's why I didn't 'ear un shut. And who may you be?'

'Well, as a matter of fact,' the gentleman told him, 'I came to see if I could interest you in a scheme.'

That was the way he talked, Bill said, as if he had taken the penthouse with the big windows and the two private bathrooms on the roof of the mainland hotel.

'It's no way to begin by leaving doors open,' Bill grumbled at him.

'But I assure you, my dear sir, I did not use the door.'

'Then 'ow did you get in?'

'I'm not here really,' said the gentleman. 'You're only seeing me.'

Bill thought that was reasonable enough, for he knew that there was not a stranger on the island and that the

95

launch from the mainland hadn't found a single passenger to face the sea which was running down the strait.

'Then if you ain't here,' he said, 'you can bugger off again.'

Bill was close on seventy and inclined to be short with people who came messing around his cottage, for he had got set in his ways – such as putting his gear and dirty dishes on the bed and sleeping on the floor because it saved trouble. A good fisherman he was, but what with the trawlers sweeping up the inshore grounds he never could catch enough to satisfy his simple tastes for beer and tobacco. He was brought up in the days when threepence bought a pint of one and an ounce of the other.

'That's no way to talk, Mr Hackafree,' the visitor complained, 'and not what I would have expected from you.'

'No call for 'ard feelings,' said Bill, for even if the chap wasn't there himself he might have a fill of baccy on him that was.

'Which is what I have come about,' replied the gentleman just as if he had read Bill's thoughts. 'May I venture to hope that you meant it when you declared shortly before my arrival that you would be eternally damned if you could find a fill at the bottom of your pouch?'

'I don't rightly know if I meant it, sir,' Bill answered, seeing that he ought to be a bit more respectful, 'but there ain't no sense in nothing these days and that's a fact.'

'You won't have to sign any papers as you do at the Post Office,' the visitor said. 'You tell me here and now that I can have the rest of you which isn't in the churchyard, and you won't want for a pint or a fill as long as you live.'

Bill was English and so were all the sixty-two inhabitants of Herbrandsholm although the island was off the coast of Wales. If this had happened among Welshmen they would have started to sing hymns and foam at the mouth instead of accepting the devil sensibly and making the most of the opportunity.

'Don't change much, do yer?' Bill asked, to give himself time to think.

The gentleman explained that his usual representatives could get all they wanted without the prospect ever noticing that he had done any business at all. But, speaking for himself, he preferred honest dealings between man and man and it had seemed to him that Herbrandsholm on a stormy night would offer a chance to keep his hand in just like old times.

Bill saw what he meant, for they were always being told that Herbrandsholm was still in the Middle Ages. The county education officer said so and the man from the Ministry of Agriculture and the sanitary inspector. You never know how far a remark like that can travel.

'Would it be all right down there where you come from?' Bill asked.

'It's what you make of it. First impressions are a lot more favourable than they used to be.'

'There's nothing else you could do with, is there? That's a fine old Welsh dresser you're a-leaning on.'

'It's as fine a piece as ever I saw,' the chap admitted. 'But it's too big to go in the launch and you know that as well as I do, Mr Hackafree.'

Bill did. That was why he still had it. Everything else had been pawned with old Timothy at the port on the mainland – his stuffed raven in the glass case and his grandfather's watch and the tea-set his aunt had left him and all the blankets which hadn't got holes in them.

In spite of his needs Bill didn't like to disappoint the vicar – old Bert, as they called him – who set an infinite value on their souls. Every Sunday for fifty years the Reverend Bertram West had put on his oilskins and stowed his gear in the locker and set out across the strait for their little bit of a church; and as if he had never enough of it he bought a cottage on the island when he retired so as to keep an eye on them and enjoy their affection.

'I ain't going to sell you what you want,' Bill said firmly. 'But I tell you what I *will* do, seeing as 'ow you've come all this way. You give me twenty pound on it like old Timothy would, and I'll take it out again when I 'ave the money.'

The gentleman seemed a bit doubtful.

'You wouldn't like to go 'ome,' Bill went on to encourage him, 'and own up to them young representatives that you've done no new business at all, would you?'

'Well, it's a deal, Mr Hackafree,' he said. 'But it's only fair to warn you that you will not have twenty quid when the time is up because there will be a late spring and a wet summer and mighty few visitors in Herbrandsholm.'

'I'll take my chance on that,' replied Bill, for even without tourists he could always count on the lobsters. 'Now, how will I give it to you?'

'Just hand it in at Old Timothy's pawnshop before midday tomorrow,' the gentleman told him, 'and I'll have a word with him meanwhile. He hasn't got a soul at all, so he will play fair with both of us.'

In the morning the sea had gone down, and Bill Hackafree rowed himself over to the mainland and tied up at the Market Steps; then he walked along the quay to Fleming Street where Timothy had kept a pawnshop for the last thirty years, to oblige seamen in need, and his father before him.

'I've got something for you, but I don't rightly know how to hand it over,' said Bill, when he had shut the door behind him and was alone with old Timothy in the little wooden pledge office. A lovely bit of panelling it was.

'That's all arranged, Bill,' Timothy assured him, 'just as soon as you put them twenty quid in your pocket, I'll have it.'

'You'll look after it, mister, won't you?' Bill asked a little anxiously, for he did not want it put among all the old junk in the window and sold by mistake.

'I'll keep it safe up there in its own basket,' said Timothy, pointing to a wide shelf at the back of the office where, for as long as any customers could remember, he stored a dusty collection of cannibal wickerwork, spears, paddles, charms and ghost masks. 'And you'll be protected by the law for one year and seven days; but if the pledge ain't redeemed by then I'll have to let him have it.'

Bill Hackafree made that twenty quid last, and it added a deal of comfort to his evenings. But nothing else would

go right for him. Summer was wet and autumn stormy, and
the lobsters kept out of Bill's pots as if the devil was at the
bottom of them. When the year and seven days were nearly
up he half thought of putting his case to the vicar; but old
Bert had done so much for the island in youth and age that
Bill did not like to upset him, for he was ninety-two and
failing fast.

Even on his boat Bill could not raise twenty quid since
he was the only chap who could keep her afloat at all. He
had nothing in the world but his old age pension, and when
he went to draw his week's money Peter Tollar, the post-
master, could not pay him because he had no cash in the
office.

'You been backing horses with Her Majesty's money
again?' Bill asked him.

'I promised I wouldn't and I haven't,' Peter Tollar said.
'It was the dogs this time. And I'll get six months at the
sessions if I get a day.'

'Nothing you could take round to Timothy?' Bill asked,
for it was never any good being angry with Peter Tollar.

'Nothing that my old woman wouldn't notice.'

It was not likely she would notice a little thing like Peter
Tollar's soul so Bill Hackafree told him how he had got out
of his own difficulties.

'Now, I'll tell you what we can do, Peter,' he went on.
'We'll put yours in and we'll take mine out. How much have
you borrowed, as it might be, from the Post Office?'

'Thirty pound,' said Peter, as near ashamed as Bill had
ever seen him.

'Well, that's thirty for you and I need twenty more to
take mine out. Suppose we ask Timothy for sixty. That'll
give us ten quid over and we'll split it.'

Peter Tollar of course would not believe him, so Bill
rowed him across to the mainland then and there. Timothy
could see nothing unbusiness-like in the transaction and said
he had been authorised to lend to any reasonable amount.
He paid out the sixty to Peter Tollar in clean pound notes
and Peter gave Bill Hackafree twenty-five of them. Bill

handed over twenty of them to Timothy, took his soul out of pawn again and put the change in his pocket.

That was a lesson to Peter Tollar, for they got back to the island just ahead of the morning launch, and a Post Office inspector stepped ashore from it all ready to audit the cash.

Peter could never keep his mouth shut; so the good news spread around among a few friends who had all grown old together and were not pestered by any young fools telling them how they ought to manage their money since the Herbrandsholm children all took jobs on the mainland as soon as they grew up.

Bill and the rest were careful to keep the secret among themselves; but what with one buying a new boat and another starting to grow daffodils on his twenty acres and Solomon Titheroe sending off his clever son to be trained as a boat-builder, it was not long before Miss Fanshawe heard a rumour of how they were coming by the money.

'Now is there a word of truth in all this?' she asked Bill Hackafree when he was spreading a load of seaweed on her asparagus bed.

'Well, m'lady, I couldn't rightly say as I believe it myself, not to swear by it,' Bill told her. 'But I got the money like the gentleman promised me, and all the rest of us too. And as it stands at the moment Solomon Titheroe 'as his soul in for six hundred pound, and you can ask of 'im if you don't believe me.'

'Then, Mr Hackafree, you will escort me to this so-called pawn-shop,' she said.

Bill was old-fashioned and he did not think Timothy's was a proper place for her. For one thing, the Fanshawes had held Herbrandsholm against the Welsh for the last thousand years, though the barbican was all they had left to show for it; and, for another, she was still a young lady of fifty.

'If it will do for you, it will do for me,' she answered, standing no nonsense from Bill. 'And I will tell you what I have told no one yet, Mr Hackafree. I owe a thousand pounds for income tax which my poor, dear father did not find it necessary to pay because he hoped they did not know they were entitled to it. And I can't pay and they're going to sell me up.'

Bill Hackafree knew nothing about income tax, but he reckoned they would all rather have Fanshawes at Herbrandsholm manor than the Inland Revenue. So he borrowed a red cushion for his boat and started up the outboard motor which he had bought with the small commissions he used to take on new business and ran Miss Fanshawe over to the mainland. Timothy looked serious but after shutting himself up for five minutes in the back office where he kept the telephone he paid Miss Fanshawe one thousand six hundred pounds with no fuss at all. She gave him back six hundred to take Solomon Titheroe's pledge out of pawn and left her own.

'I feel terrible,' she said when they were outside. 'If you will be so good as to fetch me a large Madeira from the bar, Mr Hackafree, I shall sit down in the garden of the hotel a minute. And what will you take yourself?'

When she had recovered she walked straight round to the office of the Inland Revenue and paid out the thousand in cash. That was where she made a mistake. Month after month the Inspector bothered her with letters asking her how she came by it; he reckoned that if she had made enough money to pay his tax demand she ought to pay tax on the money she had made.

Miss Fanshawe couldn't give him any explanation, and every time she swore it was capital not income the Inspector insisted that she should prove it. She broke down and took to her bed with a nurse in attendance and the doctor calling every day.

It had never occurred to any of the old fellows who had been doing business with Timothy that they might go and die before the year and seven days were up. They did not hold with dying till they were tired of living; and with all that cash flowing they were not tired of it at all. Miss Fanshawe's illness reminded them of the terms of the bargain. They were determined to get her soul out of pawn at once, even though the doctor told them that there was no immediate cause for alarm.

They held a private meeting below the quay at low tide but all the cash they could scrape together in this awkward emergency was ninety-seven pounds. When they called on Timothy he was no help. He said that his principal had so far made a loss on the deal and would not entertain any more advances on security of that nature. That was government policy, too, he told them.

There was nothing else for it but to ask old Bert's advice; and Solomon Titheroe, who was a churchwarden, had a word with him when he was helping him home after matins. Solomon expected him to say that the story was all nonsense – not that the vicar was an unbelieving sort of man, but religion is one thing and plain fact quite another.

Old Bert listened till he was safely home and back in his bed.

'Solomon, you and Bill Hackafree must tell this Timothy that I am going to put my soul in and take Miss Fanshawe's out, and see that you bring him here with two thousand pounds in cash. The devil doesn't like changing with the times any more than we do, and he will be sure to reckon a priest's soul as worth more than a layman's.'

'We all hope that you'll be with us a long time yet, sir,' said Solomon a bit anxiously.

'That's very kind of you, old friend,' the vicar replied. 'But you know and I know that I shall not be with you next Sunday, which will put an end to these irregularities once and for all.'

Solomon Titheroe did as he was told though the wind was getting up against the tide; and he and Bill Hackafree brought Timothy across to Herbrandsholm with a bag full of money padlocked to his wrist.

'What was the arrangement with your principal, Timothy?' old Bert asked when all three of them were at his bedside.

'He was to take over any pledge which was not redeemed, sir,' Timothy answered. 'But he can't touch it before the

statutory period of one year and seven days because it would
be against the law and I'd lose my licence.'

'That's just as I remember it when I was young,' said the
Reverend Bertram. 'Now you pass over that two thousand
and make a note that I give your principal the security he
requires. I shall pay you sixteen hundred back to release
Miss Fanshawe and, since one may as well be damned for
a sheep as a lamb, Mr Titheroe will take the balance of four
hundred for the Church Roof Fund.

'But I warn you, Timothy, that I won't last even the seven
days, and that gives me a whole year in your basket before
you must deliver me to your principal. It's not a place my
soul would choose for prayer,' he sighed, 'but I have been
told to fear no evil, and I have faith that before time is up
there will be no need of money to redeem the pledge.'

Space Fiction

Pepe de Cea must have remembered that I was born in
Argentina and could communicate with Spanish-speaking
horses. I was also the only one of his intimate friends likely
to be at home and in bed at 1.30 a.m. He did not even
apologise for his arrival.

'It's my mother-in-law again,' he explained. 'And I will
not calm myself. And I do not need a drink. Get dressed
and come!'

'Oh, God! Not donkeys?'

'A mule. When I came home it was in the courtyard.'

Mrs Fellowes had a vague and gossamer charm. Her
daughter, Barbara, who had impulsively married Pepe when
he was a minor attaché in the London Embassy, inherited
the charm and added the assurance proper to a young
Spanish matron. Pepe adored the pair of them and
welcomed the frequent visits of his mother-in-law to
Madrid, although on occasion he had to explain her peculi-
arities to the police. Nothing could shake Mrs Fellowes'
belief that Spaniards were cruel to animals. She had a habit
of wandering about the more primitive quarters of the city –
since animals had pretty well disappeared from the glittering
centre – with a bag of carrots and breathless rebukes.

'She hasn't stolen it?' I asked.

'She says it chased her home trying to bite her.'

'What is she doing about it?'

'Nothing. It terrified her. She has gone to bed, more
convinced than ever that my cruel countrymen brutalise
their animals with whips and red-hot pokers.'

'And Barbara?'

'Barbara is with her. In the way of women they have both
decided it is all my fault.'

104

'I don't see how it could be. You were out.'

'That's why.'

'Well, shoo the mule away!'

'I can't. You never saw such a vicious-looking brute. I think its mother was a hyaena. Its ears are about half a metre long and it bares its teeth at me.'

'Any flame from its nostrils?'

'Not yet. But don't light a match when it snorts at you!'

I had no experience of mules, only knowing that some of them can kick forwards, which a horse usually can't, and that the seat of one's pants is by no means safe even when holding the head. Still, it seemed a simple matter to accompany an unduly nervous friend and remove the beast. Other complications he would have to settle himself. The mule's proprietor might turn out to be an angrily obstinate carter who would refuse compensation and insist on an official complaint. The worst risk was what Mrs Fellowes would say in court if the police ran her in. No magistrate was going to take a lenient view after being lectured on his compatriot's supposed cruelty to animals.

Pepe's seventeenth-century house was in an unfashionable district off the Atocha, but within its courtyard he had the quiet and privacy of a village. He parked his flashy sports car in the street and we entered the court through a narrow archway. The mule was standing on the cobbles – a huge, black draught mule, a mediaeval gargoyle of a mule. Half a wooden post dangled from its halter. Its tail was bald except for an obscene tuft at the end. Its snarling teeth were bright yellow in the light over the front door and quite long enough for any reasonable hyaena.

'It pulled that post down for the sake of carrots?' I asked.

'Or to attack my mother-in-law. When they met, it was tied up in front of a tavern with the cart alongside.'

'Well, we'd better start with some more carrots.'

Edging past the mule, Pepe disappeared into the house. He returned with only two carrots, saying that he couldn't find any more in the larder. I sent him back to forage for something else and to assure his women, if they came down, that I would handle the problem without unnecessary viol-

105

ence. I certainly was not going to force that mule to do anything against its wishes.

I advanced upon it, preceded by the longest carrot. One ear was reassuringly forward; the other was half way down its neck, apparently investigating sounds from the broken pillar. It accepted the carrot with a snort and a start as if it had been dreaming of the things and suddenly found they were a real presence.

With head and neck aligned like a striking snake and baring its fearful yellow teeth it proceeded to examine me. I stood still only because I did not dare to turn my back. Its oddly prehensile nose was velvet and friendly. Its brown eyes, though mischievous, were showing no white. When I found that it enjoyed being patted and talked to, I realised that the fighting-stallion effect was artificial. That mule had been deliberately taught to smile – either to keep off thieves or, more probably, to earn free drinks for its owner. Quite obviously it had been treated with affection as one of the family. But the family was poor. Carrots had seldom come its way. Its intent in breaking loose and chasing Mrs Fellowes into a smart trot had been to get some more from her bag.

Pepe, returning from the house with a long parcel in greaseproof paper, was impressed. If he had been brought up among horses he would soon have seen, as I did, that this hideous monstrosity was as friendly as a child's pony. But I did not disturb his opinion of me and asked him what he had in the parcel.

'*Brazos de Gitana*,' he replied. 'It was all I could find. Barbara is giving a party tomorrow. Do you think he'll like it?'

I said it would certainly be new to him. There were over a couple of feet of this delectable cake, somewhat resembling a Swiss Roll and stuffed with gently foaming cream. I tried a piece on the mule. I doubt if he found it as welcome as carrots, but it was an agreeable change from hay and the remains of the family's chick-peas. He faced it boldly and with growing interest like a man trying out a first-class French restaurant with a lunch voucher.

'Do you think you can entice him back with that?' Pepe asked.

'I think *we* can. Where to?'

'She isn't quite sure. You know how she wanders about dreaming that she is St Francis. She believes the tavern was somewhere between the Atocha station and the Plaza de la Cebada.'

They were the best part of a mile from each other. We were bound to attract a following of idle and interested spectators while leading a draught mule on a random search through the back streets of Madrid. Pepe could not be anything but a young and monied *señorito* and I am always recognised as English.

'Have you decided what we are going to say to the police?' I asked him, removing the length of worm-eaten post from the mule's halter. It was deeply carved and suggested the pillar of a verandah rather than a mere hitching post.

'We just found it wandering. And you with British public spirit and responsibility . . .'

'On the contrary. You, Pepe, with the splendid and generous impulse of a Spaniard . . .'

'Suppose you ride it?' he suggested.

I pointed out that there was no reason to believe the mule had ever been ridden and that it was a long way to the ground. If we had a cart, we might drive it.

The mention of wheels brought Pepe back to the automobile age.

'I'll run down to the Atocha goods yard and hire a cattle truck,' he said. 'There's sure to be one about and we'll only need it for ten minutes.'

That was probable. The tavern and deserted cart could not be far away since the mule seemed to have vanished round corners and into Pepe's courtyard before anyone could spot what had happened and take off after it.

When he had left, the night wore on for me and my peaceable companion. In the street outside there was even an hour of silence. I supplied the mule with a bucket of water and another mouthful of cream and sponge cake. He then went to sleep on his feet; so did I on the front steps, for I felt reluctant to ring the bell and wake up the house just to tell Barbara and Mrs Fellowes that their mule at present was contented and affectionate. While the future was uncertain, witnesses were better away.

About four in the morning Pepe silently free-wheeled into the courtyard, taking the corner with the skill of long practice.

'Got one!' he exclaimed. 'There was nothing at the station, so I had to go down to the slaughterhouse. I found a man who had just delivered some cattle and was glad to have the job.'

'Did you tell him what it was?'

'Only to move a beast to the Atocha station.'

A dilapidated van backed up to the archway which was too low for it to enter the court. The driver came round and let down the tailboard to form a ramp. He was a real sun-dried tough from Burgos. He said that if he had expected a mule, which he hadn't, it should not be one frothing at the mouth. God knows what he did expect! Livestock in the centre of Madrid must be rare.

I had no time to explain that the froth was whipped cream, for the mule panicked. Evidently it had never travelled in a van. It folded its ears back and flung up its gaunt, black head to have a better look, nearly lifting me off the ground. The man from Burgos circled cautiously round it and caught it a whack with his stick which would have earned him a lecture from Mrs Fellowes. The mule, too, was scandalised by this normal method of starting nervous cattle up a ramp. It bucked and let go with its off hind leg. Not viciously. It was only protesting against such treatment when out of harness. That hoof fairly whistled past the driver's stomach; the head then twisted right round at an unnatural angle to inspect him.

I entered the van with the sticky parcel of *Brazos de Gitana*. That was effective. The mule bared its yellow fangs in the usual smile and clattered up the ramp at me. I tied it up while it lovingly filled my ear with cream. The driver had taken refuge in his cab; so I closed up the tailboard and joined Pepe in the front seat.

The driver was crossing himself. I think it may have
occurred to him that we had just exorcised the old house
and that this grinning 'weremule' was the result. He was
in a nightmare anyway. Nothing made sense. When Pepe
directed him to the station and then, as soon as we were
safely away from home, turned him off to the Cebada
through a labyrinth of one-way streets, he shrugged his
shoulders and gave it up.

It did not take us long to discover the mule's starting
point: a little square with a patch of paving in the middle
on which were some empty carts. Outside a tavern was a
narrow verandah with a sagging roof. One of its supporting
columns was broken. An old-fashioned carter was being
supported by the tavern keeper and his fellows while two
policemen tried to take notes of his remarks. He was magnificently in liquor. So, I think, were the rest of them. If they
had only recently noticed the absence of the mule, it stood
to reason.

Fortunately we were loitering along the opposite side of
the square, too far away for the driver to hear what all the
excitement was about. Pepe snapped at him to turn right
and so startled the man that he did. We bounced the wrong
way up a one-way street, straightened ourselves out and
were compelled to arrive at the Puerta del Sol.

'And now?' the driver asked, pulling up right in the centre
of Madrid.

'Straight on,' said Pepe confidently.

There was really no straight on; but the man from Burgos
took it that he should continue north – which he did, looking
more and more suspicious, until there was little of Madrid
left. We could not discuss in his presence what on earth we
were to do. We did not dare to tip the mule out into the
road in front of a witness who knew Pepe's address and was
certain to talk.

'To whom does this animal belong?' the driver asked
sullenly.

'Friend, it belongs to us both,' Pepe answered.

'Then listen, both of you! I am not a man for jokes. The
transport of cattle is my living. There are inspections. There

are licences. What we are going to do is to stop at the nearest police station.'

I foresaw no trouble in clearing myself of the charge of stealing a mule; but Spanish summary justice is slow, and it would be at least a month before my passport was returned and I was formally congratulated on my innocence. As for Pepe, he could only denounce his mother-in-law's habits and opinions – which would not lead to peace at home – or pay an immense fine as a gilded youth who had amused himself at the expense of the public.

The mention of licences worked on his despairing imagination. He said:

'As you like. It's not our fault that the chap we expected never turned up. To us the police can do nothing.'

'Nor to me.'

'If God wills. I don't know the regulations of the Veterinary Service.'

'What have the vets to do with it?'

'*Hombre*! You don't think I would get rid of a family pet for no reason?'

'Family pet, my foot!'

'You cannot imagine how fond of it my father was,' Pepe protested, looking hurt. 'And now it has to be put down.'

'What's the matter with it?'

'Well you saw how it attacked with open mouth this gentleman whom it has known since it was a foal. In all fairness I must advise you to disinfect your van.'

'Jesus! I have children at home!'

'There's nothing to worry about. It hasn't bitten you. You have only to keep your trap shut.'

'I'm not going another step,' said the driver, stopping abruptly in a melancholy nowhere intensified by the first grey of dawn.

'But I could not know you had children. Then we have only to settle accounts. We have come six times the distance you expected, so I'll make it six times the price. Agreed?'

'Since I am on my way home anyway, I won't say no. But for the sake of us all, not a word!' the driver added anxiously. 'If this came out, they could order my van to be burned.'

Pepe gave him his solemn promise to keep quiet and we both had the effrontery to shake his hand.

There was no time to waste. The streets would soon be stirring. We stopped and unloaded in the first private spot we could see: a blind alley between a wall and the blank side of a narrow, isolated tenement house. I felt it a low trick to abandon this accomplished animal so far from home, but the police would soon identify it and meanwhile there was plenty of garbage for its entertainment. When the driver had reversed into the cover of the alley, the mule clattered down upon the concrete, ears forward and delighted to see me again. As soon as I had replaced the tailboard, the van gave one leap towards Burgos and disappeared.

Leaving the mule with one ear exploring the silence and the other twitching above a rubbish bin, Pepe and I tip-toed away. We had just turned the corner into the street when we heard it walking after us. I think it was not the first time the mule had been lost, and it had learned from experience – for all the horse species are nervous creatures and remember panic – that when on its own it became an outlaw hateful to human beings instead of a hard-working family friend. Pepe and I represented not only *Brazos de Gitana* but security.

The only escape route was through the front door of the tenement house and up the first flight of concrete steps. The mule stood outside extending its monstrous ears in our direction like the antennae of a visiting Martian. It would have heard nothing but the vague noises of early workers about to tumble out of bed if Pepe had not nervously started up another flight.

His footsteps were enough. The mule tripped quietly and confidently up the stairs and arrived on the landing with every sign of lasting affection and its nose in my pocket looking for crumbs. Finding no more sponge cake it started off after Pepe in the hope that he might have a bit left.

Pepe still did not understand those bared teeth. He dashed upstairs making far more noise than the careful mule which must have been bred from a mountain pack donkey. When all three of us were at last reunited we found we were on the fifth and last landing. The flats below were stirring but without excitement. A door shut. Two men exchanged good mornings. The day's work had started.

The mule remained as still as we. If my theory is correct, he had caught the smell of our anxiety and assumed that we too were hiding from the public hostility which descended on him whenever his master, who should never have taught him to smile, spent long and forgetful hours in Madrid taverns.

When all was comparatively quiet again and later risers had pulled the blankets over their ears, I tried to persuade the mule to accompany me downstairs and into the open. He didn't like it. He wouldn't have it. The treads were narrow and a hoof slipped. He backed cautiously onto the landing again.

'That's fixed him,' Pepe said. 'Now all we have to do is to run.'

I refused to risk damaging a valuable animal which had put its mistaken trust in his mother-in-law. If deserted it might impulsively decide to follow at any cost and break a leg or its neck or probably both. I reminded Pepe that we had set out with the intention of returning stolen goods.

'But we can't just stay here!' he screamed in a whisper.

There was something in that. Front doors might open at any minute. A sense of humour was too much to expect so early in the morning. We should be shouted down by all the inhabitants of the building and, as news of the mule spread, by those of the neighbouring tenement houses as well.

On this top floor were two apartments, one occupied and one still to let. Between them a half flight of steps continued up to a little penthouse in which was a wooden door giving access to the flat roof and the washing-lines. I suggested that we should go up and see if there was anywhere to hide.

'Suppose the mule comes too?'

Any fool could see it was impossible, I replied. The door

was smaller than a standard door and manifestly too low for the mule to pass through.

But he could and he did tackle the flight of steps. It was amazing how that great, satanic, black brute could step so daintily. Approaching from below, at an angle of forty-five degrees to the horizontal, his head and neck of course went through the door easily, and before we could shut it. He liked what he saw and he liked us. He stretched out his forelegs alongside his neck and gave a heave with his hind. The door frame shuddered in its plaster, and he was through. He was on the roof.

It was near sunrise. We could see the range of the Guadarrama and the distant, fortunate traffic on the road to Burgos. I hoped the mule would be patient and enjoy the view, but it was thirsty and smelling water it reared up with no more trouble than a black cat, forelegs upon the roof tank, prodigiously outlined against the dawn. We crept away and bolted the door behind us after removing a few tell-tale black hairs from the lintel.

We were just about to sneak down the stairs to liberty and were discussing in whispers whether we could get away with a story of having come up to visit a girl or whether no story at all would be necessary. With luck it wouldn't be; there was still no one about. And then a vast, muffled crash, without splinterings, crackings or any preliminaries, shook the top storey of that house in a single tremor.

'God help us, he's gone through the roof!' Pepe exclaimed.

We waited. Nothing happened. It was the occupied flat into which the mule had fallen, but there was no protest from the tenant. Beneath us were only some faintly audible expletives from lower flats. The inhabitants were probably accustomed to any sort of thud echoing through the whole of that cheap, shockingly built tenement house. This one could have been caused by a wardrobe collapsing or father falling off a ladder and tearing the sink out by the roots.

But one could bet that such a thump would alarm the owner if he lived on his own palsied premises. Far down the bare well of the staircase someone burst out of a flat, hammered on the opposite door and routed out a tenant who, at a guess, acted as part-time porter. Both of them started up the stairs, loudly debating about what could have tumbled down and giving us time to take refuge in a cupboard under the half-flight of steps, crouched among mops and buckets. The pair unbolted the roof door and saw at a glance that everything was standing up which should be. The side of the penthouse concealed the hole through which the mule had vanished, and naturally they were not looking for a hole since there was nothing which could have made one.

We remained where we were, panic-stricken through long minutes.

'The empty flat!' Pepe suggested at last. 'If we drop off the parapet, we'll land on the balcony.'

That was true enough, provided we did not go through it; so we tiptoed back to the roof, the landlord having left the door on the latch, but then were so flustered that we could not decide which balcony was the right one. In order to get our bearings we opened the door for a moment and looked down. It was like opening up a wasps' nest. At least six women were screaming at each other simultaneously.

The balcony of the empty flat held, though quivering as we hit it. The concrete balustrade was high enough to hide us if we squatted down and there we had to stay. The window which led into the flat was shuttered and locked.

I insisted that I was only an interested foreigner, that I would have nothing to do with forcible entry and that probably someone would come to inspect the flat during the day and let us out. Pepe replied that we might just as well add burglary to other crimes and that what bothered him even more than his diplomatic career was Barbara. If he didn't get home soon, she would assume he had been killed by her mother's mule and telephone the police.

He sat down by the shutter and began to cut away the lower slats with a pocket-knife. It was a long job; the builder's carpenter had been more conscientious than his masons. Meanwhile a small crowd gathered in the street, all talking at once, while women fluttered off to spread the

114

news to other tenements. A self-important fellow on the balcony immediately below us was conducting a conversation with two other balconies and the street.

'What's happening?' Pepe asked me, struggling to loosen slats without doing violent and audible damage.

'A lady in hysterics and a dressing gown is saying that she is a respectable woman and that her bed has hitherto remained inviolate. I suspect she was in somebody else's.'

'I am not interested in local scandal.'

'Yes, you are. She says that when she returned to her flat from an errand of mercy she found a mule in her bed. It was sleeping like a Christian with its head on her pillow. She thought it was the devil.'

'Her theology seems a bit muddled.'

'Well, one can see what she meant.'

'Have they sent for the police?'

'They have – and the Fire Brigade.'

'How do they think it got there?'

'The chap underneath is talking about a rain of frogs in his grandfather's day.'

'A café talker! Irrelevant as always!'

'No, he isn't. It's agreed all round that the mule dropped from the sky. Even if it could climb stairs, it could not get through the door. And the landlord swears that anyway the door was bolted.'

'Why the hell wasn't it hurt?' Pepe asked, wrenching free another couple of slats.

I listened until I got the public verdict. The sturdy common sense of the people had arrived at the only possible answer. The mule had come down on a parachute. On the other hand no parachute had been found. The persistent and dogmatic voice on the balcony below said that parachutes were now superseded, that his wife's cousin had told him that the Americans were experimenting with anti-gravity.

'Like monkeys,' someone answered obscurely.

'It is the Russians who use monkeys. From the Americans one can expect nothing less than a mule.'

Pepe was inclined to be anti-American, so I passed this

on to him as evidence of their unassailable prestige. At the time it did not seem to register. He lay on his back and kicked the glass out of the pane behind the slats he had removed.

'Crawl through that quick!' he ordered. 'And mind broken glass!'

We padded through two empty rooms and opened the front door a crack. Not a face was turned in our direction. The passage and living room of the opposite flat were full of tenants, whispering to each other and trying to get a glimpse of the mule. It must have been still luxuriating on the squashed bed, weary of travel and possibly smiling in its sleep. Evidently no one had the courage to wake it up.

Silently shutting the door of the flat behind us, we mingled with the overflow and started to peer over shoulders. That was a mistake. The owner of the house spotted at once that we had no right to be there. It had not occurred to us that downstairs a policeman had already been posted to keep out the curious.

'And where have you come from?' he demanded suspiciously.

'Would you be good enough to tell me where I can find the proprietor of this building?' Pepe asked.

'I am.'

Alongside the landlord was a young Spanish clerk, black-suited, trying to look experienced in such accidents.

'And this gentleman?'

'The local agent of my insurance company.'

'Then it could not be more convenient,' Pepe said with the impressive, formal courtesy of the diplomatic service. 'I am the official interpreter of the American Embassy. This is the Technical Officer. He speaks, unfortunately, little Spanish. Now, where can we talk freely?'

I was alarmed that Pepe should have deprived me of any control over whatever he was planning. However, the landlord's shabby, groundfloor flat to which he led us at least contained a much needed drink. Since we were in the respectable company of capital and insurance, the policeman in the hall ignored us.

116

'As between allies we beg for the utmost discretion,'
Pepe began. 'Now, we understand that in the course of an
experiment in the stratosphere some animal was prema-
turely released . . .'

I got it at last, and interrupted in English:

'Ask him which animal!'

Pepe did so.

'Ah, only the mule!' he exclaimed in a tone of relief. 'The
mule, yes! It was computerised for 41.63 North, 19.00 West.
A cruiser is standing by.'

'Where is that?' the insurance agent asked.

'North of the Azores. In the circumstances an unaccept-
able error.'

'But my roof!' the landlord complained. 'One does not
expect such carelessness from a great and honourable
nation.'

'That is the reason for our visit. If you and your agent
will be good enough to call at the American Embassy at
11.30 precisely and ask for the Naval Attaché, the matter
will be settled on the spot. All we require, as I said, is the
utmost discretion.'

'And what shall we do with the mule?'

'To avoid questions and to give an appearance of
normality the Minister of the Interior has suggested that the
Fire Brigade should winch it down and hand it over to the
police.'

I got up and shook hands all round.

'Your car is waiting?' the landlord asked.

'We do not leave a car in public places where it might
arouse embarrassing curiosity,' Pepe replied.

Two streets away we found a bus and were home for
breakfast. The next day's papers informed us without
comment that a mule, inexplicably discovered on an isolated
roof, had been tranquillised and removed by the Fire
Brigade and eventually restored to its owner. The incident
did not even make the front page. Of course not. Only the
improbable is news. The impossible is not.

But I could not leave it at that. I spent several evenings
haunting the Plaza de la Cebada until I came face to face

117

with that unmistakeable animal outside the same tavern and now between the shafts of a cart. Its proud possessor told me over his second litre that, by God, I was a friend and so he did not wish me to put my faith in rumours. It was quite untrue, he said, that his mule had strayed into the garden of the American Embassy and been launched into space, travelling twice round the world between midnight and dawn. No, not at all! For the sake of its smile and numerous accomplishments it had without doubt been stolen by a circus manager and escaped from the van – unhappy, loyal creature – into the nearest house.

And then a woman! Always a woman behind every commotion, true? Her husband was away, so she left the door open for her lover. And in walked Sebastiano.

The carter rose from the table, steadying himself with a hand upon my shoulder, unharnessed the mule and ordered:

'*Aupa*, Sebastiano!'

The mule obediently performed a curret and pawed the air as if trained in the Spanish Riding School. I could at last understand its apocalyptic pose against the water tank.

'So you see,' the carter went on, 'she fled in panic slamming the door and my clever Sebastiano tried to cut his way out through the ceiling. That was enough to bring the roof down. Now it can be seen how they build houses for the poor!'

The police, I gathered, had tended to approve his theory though it was hardly more believable than Pepe's impromptu space fiction. I sympathised with them. Anyone possessed by Sebastiano was bound instinctively to be in favour of ascent from hell rather than descent from heaven.

Estancia La Embajada

The mound was so regular that I could have sworn it had been built by human labour; but standing on the summit, I found that it was no vast tomb which I had climbed; it was a neat, formal and miniature volcano with a passive crater in the centre where the black lava thrust its ridges and tumours through scanty turf. The hill stood on a plain of dark green pasture, some twenty square miles in extent, surrounded by steep slopes which, on the north, mounted to the snows and smoke-plume of Cotopaxi. The valley appeared to have a single owner, for it was well fenced and drained, and all the tracks converged upon a white-walled, red-roofed house marked on the map as 'Estancia La Embajada' – Embassy Ranch. The herds of dairy cattle and the low clouds washing the sides of the bowl suggested that I was on some farmer's land in the Severn valley instead of a considerable estate ten thousand feet above the Pacific, with its own private volcano.

It was late afternoon when I got down from this savage infant of a hill. The landmarks of the cordillera were blotted out, and grey tentacles of mist were feeling for the bottom of the valley. I did not fancy the long ride back to Riobamba. The path wound along the edge of a crater lake which had startled both me and my mule in sunlight – it looked and smelt like one of the more unpleasant hazards on the course of *Pilgrim's Progress* – and was prohibitive when imagined under crawling vapour. I decided to ride over the *estancia* and ask for a bed.

We plodded through the mist and two streams. A massive Holstein bull, coloured black and white like Cotopaxi, materialised out of a cloud and accompanied us for half a mile. Neither of us liked him. True, I knew that the lean

119

beasts of real cattle country did not attack a mounted man; but I was doubtful whether this aristocrat imported from Europe would have heard of the local rule. The scent of a dairy came to my nostrils as we paced up the avenue of eucalyptus that led to the house, and when we arrived before the facade of round white arches two golden cockers barked and whined and leapt against their chains with the usual friendliness of spaniels to any newcomer. At the noise of this enthusiasm, effective as the growl of a watch-dog, a tall man in shirt-sleeves, corduroy breeches and gaiters came round the corner of the house. His face was bronzed and his hair dark and curly. He did not look like an Ecuadorian born. Possibly a Basque immigrant, I thought.

'Buenas tardes, señor,' I began. 'Excuse this visit without ceremony, but . . .'

He watched me keenly while I spoke.

'A dirty evening,' he interrupted cordially with a slight West Country burr in his voice. 'We'll gladly put you up if you care to stay the night.'

'Are you English?' I asked in surprise.

'Cornish,' he corrected me.

I put him down as a cowman or stud-groom imported by the owner of the *estancia*. It seemed odd that a man with all the earmarks of one fixed to his own soil should be earning wages in the heart of the cordillera.

'Good Lord! What's brought you out here?' I asked impulsively.

'A woman,' he chuckled.

He did not seem at all upset about her, seemed even to be mischievously waiting for some sympathetic remark from me.

An Indian in a red poncho and wide-brimmed straw hat trotted out of the damp mist, driving before him a donkey and a llama both loaded with brushwood. He was moving in the wrong dimension. The Cornishman, the spaniels, the dairy scents and the dripping trees around the house had created a complete illusion of England. I should have been less surprised to see a boy on a bicycle delivering the evening paper.

'*Tu*, Felipe!' ordered the Cornishman. 'Take the gentleman's mule round to the stables. He is staying the night.'

'*Ahora mismo, patron*,' answered the peon respectfully.

'You own this place?' I asked.

'Of course! Come in – come in!'

His manners were more brusque and free than those of an Ecuadorian, but the voice of all Spanish America rang out hospitably with his own. He led me into the hall of the *estancia*, a magnificent room with white-washed walls and Indian rugs on a floor of patterned tiles. It was too large to look untidy, though freely scattered with the possessions of a man living alone and at ease. There was a heap of saddlery under the far window, and on a long table – rough and evidently made on the estate – boxes of soil and packets of seeds and fertilisers which suggested that he had been experimenting with grasses.

'A fine place!' I said.

'Not bad is it? I don't want anything better. No summer and no winter and the best pasture in Ecuador. You should see it on a fine day.'

'I did, from the top of your hill.'

'Prospecting?' he asked coldly.

'No. Idling. I saw the hill from the head of the valley, and thought it might have been built by the old Quitos; so I rode over to look at it.'

'A-ah! I'll be bound you did! And you're not the first. George Trevithick's my name,' he added heartily, as if now satisfied by my credentials.

I introduced myself in turn.

'Well, it's luck for me that you happened to feel a bit curious about my hill,' he said. 'It's not often I get a chance to speak my own language.'

As he knotted a scarf around his throat and settled a solid, well-cut tweed coat on his broad shoulders, I looked at him more closely. He was older than I had thought at first – a man in the middle fifties, bearing himself with a distinction that might, when he was younger, have been a raffish swagger, but was now the independence of one who had made his own laws for himself and found that they also

121

appeared satisfactory to his fellows. I could not understand how I had mistaken him for the cowman. He was very obviously the *estanciero*.

He poured drinks, and we discussed Cornwall and cattle till supper. On the top of the Andes, a hundred miles from the equator, his pedigree beasts were short-lived and inclined to curious failures of their natural instincts. But he was a born experimenter, and the butter and cheese showed a profit. The religious orders of Quito – priests clucked around the capital as thick as fat black hens on a chicken farm – were, he said, his best customers.

A wizened *mestizo* in a white jacket showed us into the dining-room. It was exquisite. Plate, linen, glass and furniture would have done credit to a Spanish grandee. Over his seat hung the portrait of a woman in her early thirties: a full-bosomed commanding beauty with fiery brown eyes in an unintelligent face.

'That's her!' he said, jerking an irreverent thumb over his shoulder towards the picture. 'What do you think of her?'

I couldn't gather from his tone whether she was the chief love of his life from whom he had at last and proudly broken free, or merely some woman over whom he had triumphed.

'She had a pretty good opinion of herself,' I replied. 'And I expect she was right.'

'Ah, Doña Clara! Doña Clara!' he chuckled.

The cooking of the simple meal was excellent, and the *estanciero* was a good talker. Like so many exiles, he revelled in the expressiveness of his own language. He would halt for a moment in his flow of eloquence, feel for the English word, taste it and hand it to me, as it were, on the tip of his tongue. He had the slow, rich humour of the West Countryman, but had lived too long in Latin America to have kept a West Countryman's reserve.

'If you're idling,' he said when we had reached the coffee, 'why don't you stay a few weeks?'

'I wish I could. But I'm only idling for the weekend. I've been in Quito on business and I have to be down at Guayaquil the day after tomorrow to catch my boat. I'm staying three nights at Riobamba on the way to get some exercise and see a bit more of the plateau.'

'Three nights at Riobamba!' he laughed. 'You must be the first person that has ever stayed more than one in that hotel!'

An exaggeration, of course, but there can't have been many. The train from Quito to Guayaquil stopped for the night at Riobamba, and the hotel lived on passengers who arrived at seven in the evening and left at six next morning. That one ate reasonably and slept in a clean bed was proof of the proprietor's natural hospitality; he could neither reduce the number of his guests by a bad name, nor increase them by a good one.

'The hotel's all right,' I said, 'considering . . .'

'All right? You bet it's all right! I bless that hotel. Good Lord, I – I turn to it to pray!'

He looked at me sardonically, as if measuring how much curiosity so deliberate a statement had aroused.

'Is that where you met Doña Clara?' I asked.

'No. I met her just five hours before we got there – when the consul escorted me to the train. A polite man, the consul. He didn't quite know where he stood, you see.'

'With Doña Clara?'

'With me. I was being shown the door – though I paid my own first-class fare and had my steamship ticket. He had word that I wasn't to be allowed to tender for the army contracts.'

'Rifles?'

'God, no! Rubber goods. There'd been a bit of a stink about them in Bogota. They were rotten, and unfortunately somebody opened the cases before I could put my next deal through at Quito. Pennyfather – that's the consul – had had a letter, one of those marked confidential with the lion and the unicorn shouting secrets at each other across the top. He said he didn't want to tell the War Ministry about me, but that he would if I didn't clear out.

'We were late arriving at the station. The consul had given me lunch. He was very friendly once it had been decided that I'd go quietly. He'd been in business himself.

'You know the first-class coach that goes down to Guayaquil three times a week. It was the same one in those days – the same ten armchairs mounted on swivels so that you can turn round and talk to your three nearest fellow passengers. Like a little club for bishops and landowners.

'There were only two travellers going down to the coast, though what with all the fuss and baggage it looked as if half Quito were travelling with them. Doña Clara was saying goodbye. Her servants were weeping – though I'll bet they were glad to be rid of her – and her friends and her enemies and the stationmaster and the porters were rushing in and out of the coach. That woman and her stuff were all over the place.

'Tucked away behind a pile of suitcases was her husband, Don Anastasio. He was taking his wife for a holiday by the same boat I was bound north on. He was the vice-president of the republic at the time. There was a senator sitting on each arm of his chair and all their three heads were wagging together. They were pretending to be occupied with last-minute affairs of state, and actually protecting themselves against Doña Clara. I tell you there was more cackle going on round that first-class coach than the two others.'

This was a good illustration, for the two coaches next to the locomotive were always crammed with Indians and *mestizos*, passengers overflowing onto the platform, onlookers overflowing into the train. The railway still held romance and a journey by it was an excuse for a family gathering. Even a traveller to one of the little country towns of the plateau, a day's ride on a horse, was seen off by all his relations if he took the train.

'The consul just had time to introduce me to the pair of them. I wasn't popular with Doña Clara, but Don Anastasio was cordial. He was glad to see me. It meant he wouldn't have to listen to his wife all the way to Guayaquil.

'Pennyfather had no sooner seen me into the train than it jerked. You know that jerk. It's the only way to clear the coaches of non-travellers. They don't pay any attention to the conductor or the whistle or the station bell, but the false start tumbles them out like fleas off the back of a dog. The

124

train travels about two feet and then stops. It doesn't really leave for another thirty seconds.

'Well, Doña Clara spent the thirty seconds bowing and smiling to all the human souls she had incommoded, and giving Pennyfather dirty looks. She didn't pay much attention to small fry such as consuls. She liked ministers. And as Great Britain didn't have a minister in Ecuador, she was all the more annoyed with Pennyfather. Besides, she thought it was pretty poor taste on his part to stick a friend on the train when she wanted it to herself.

'You should have seen that coach when we pulled out of Quito. There wasn't a seat and hardly standing room in the aisle. Two chairs were occupied by the vice-president and his missus, three by her flowers, four by her baggage, and on the tenth she had a regular wardrobe of wraps and coats, with a damn great garden-party hat on top of the lot which I guessed she meant to put on five minutes before we reached Guayaquil. I didn't like messing her things about, so I smiled at her sort of helplessly. But she looked clean through me. Don Anastasio caught my eye, and got up to clear the chair alongside his own.

' "Not that one," says she (Trevithick imitated the deep voice of a pompous woman and made me howl with laughter). "You may move the flowers, Anastasio."

'Don Anastasio sighed – well, no! He'd never have dared to sigh in front of his wife. It would have started an argument. Put it this way. He looked as if he had sighed. The flowers were easy enough to move, but at the other end of the coach. She had banished me as far away as possible.

'We moved them, and then Don Anastasio silently shook my hand. I couldn't quite understand it at the time. He told me afterwards that the scent of all those flowers had reminded him of the innumerable funerals that a vice-president had to attend. He was just keeping his mind off everything – trying to get away from Doña Clara and travel and the reproaches he'd have to listen to as far as Riobamba – and so he was open to the suggestion of funerals, if you see what I mean. He shook my hand quite automatically. I was the chief mourner.

'Well, I returned his grip – with sympathy, for I was thinking of Doña Clara. He knew that all right. To cover his embarrassment he wiped up the damp patches which the flowers had left on the cream-coloured upholstery, and spread his mackintosh for me to sit on. Then he patted me on the back – he was a great back-patter, Don Anastasio – and returned to his place.

'I sat there, looking out of the window and watching Ecuador slide past. I wasn't feeling very bright. You know how it is. If one has a few drinks and a good lunch and then gets on a train or boat – down come all the sins you've ever committed, and your last sin in particular. And, what's worse, all the damn futility of living the way you do, or living at all if it comes to that. Hell! I've known men whose memories were fair stuffed with sins and thought none the worse of them. We wouldn't know what sin was if it weren't for the priests and the lawyers. But we'd know futility all right. I tell you, I think sometimes that monkeys know all about futility. That's why they're always hopping after some mischief; they daren't do nothing. I'm going to buy a monkey some day. It's no good theorising and reading about human beings. I sit here in the evenings and think I've solved the problems of the universe, but it's all hot air. There's no solid fact behind it. I must buy a monkey. I say, where was I?'

'You were watching Ecuador slide past the window,' I said.

'Ah, yes. Well, I liked Ecuador – green and soft and warm. I was sick at being turned out of it. It reminded me of home. My father was a farmer – a gentleman farmer he called himself, but the only gentlemanliness I saw was when he used to swear at me and my brothers for running around with the village kids. I did a bunk when I was sixteen. South Africa, South America, New South Wales – always South Something-or-other I've been in. Always running around to make a bit of money, enough to move somewhere else.

'That's what I was thinking as we joggled along the Altiplano from Quito to Riobamba. It was a bad five hours – I expect you've had 'em too – but something came out of it.

126

I discovered that all the time I had been wanting a farm without my father.

'Of course I could have had a farm without my father any year in the last twenty when I was flush. But it hadn't occurred to me. Farms and fathers – they went together in my mind. I saw they needn't necessarily go together. And I knew where I wanted my farm, too. Up here. None of your tropics and deserts for me. I like grass.

'I didn't give my fellow-passengers another thought. I didn't want to talk, nor did they. When we got to Riobamba I gave them a nod and strolled over to the hotel carrying my own bag. That seems unlikely, I know, considering all the boys in town earn their pocket-money at the station. But they were busy struggling for Doña Clara's baggage and, when they got it, arguing about who should carry what. She disorganised that station good and proper, and then put the hotel out of action by having everything she possessed taken up to her room. After that she abode by her stuff, like the chap in the Bible.

'As soon as the hall was clear I made tracks for the bar to see if I couldn't shake that depression. I had perched myself on a high stool before I saw Don Anastasio. He was hiding behind a palm-tree at the side of the door into the hall, so that anyone looking through could honestly say they hadn't seen him. He had a whisky and soda in a pint glass on the table at his side. A good rich yellow it was, too. It was mixed about half and half – as I found out when I tasted the one he ordered for me.

'Yes, he waved me into the next chair as soon as our eyes met. That's why I bless that hotel. If I hadn't come down to the bar just then, I might be – well, anywhere to-day. Clerking it in Costa Rica, for example, and stealing enough from my boss to get tight every night.

'We had a couple of drinks together, and he asked me what I was doing in Ecuador and how I liked it. I couldn't tell him the truth. He'd have laughed probably, but I was too ashamed of it myself. I'd never been ordered out of a country before, you see. I'd deserved it several times – plenty of times! But it hadn't actually happened. It takes a fact to make my conscience work. I suppose that's so for most people. We think ourselves bloody angels until the judge hands out a sentence of five years' hard, and then we see what we really are.

'I told Don Anastasio that I'd been up and down the coast for years without ever visiting Quito, and that I'd come up to have a look at it – which was true so far as it went. I said I liked it best of all the republics. That pleased him. And what pleased him still more was that I treated him with proper respect. He was a jolly fellow of about my own age, but that was no reason for forgetting he was a vice-president. Don't think I'm a snob, but I've been knocking around South America long enough to enjoy calling a man Excellency if he's entitled to it. And Don Anastasio was. He was one of the old sort, rich as they make 'em, and free and easy in his ways. He looked taller than his height, for he had a fine head on him with a wavy, pointed brown beard and a moustache that didn't go up nor down, but straight out to the sides in two soft even waves. Gallant – that's the word for his face. A man you liked at first sight, with a twinkle in his eyes when he wasn't looking at Doña Clara.'

'Where is he now?' I asked.

'Gone off as a diplomat. His party was thrown out in the last revolution, but he always gets a job. Everyone likes him, so they see that his missus has something to keep her quiet.

'Well, after a bit he asked me if I'd care to join them at dinner. I said I feared the *señora* would be too tired for a guest. I thought, you see, that she'd probably object. I'd misjudged Don Anastasio there. He was much too polite to ask a chap to sit down with his wife unless he knew she would approve. He wasn't afraid of her; he was just too damned courteous. It came to the same in the end.

'Don Anastasio insisted. She had said, it seemed, that I looked very distinguished and that she was glad Pennyfather had introduced me. I expect that, like most women, she'd been piqued at my making no advances though she was ready enough to snub me if I did.

'She was very cordial at dinner. She let me know that she didn't usually entertain people she met on trains, but was graciously pleased to make an exception. Doña Clara wasn't inhospitable – so long as you showed you were impressed by her as a hostess. And that was easy. She was a beauty. The more exasperated with her you were, the more you wanted to wake her up. She made you understand how it is men can beat their wives when they wouldn't beat a dog.

Don Anastasio got us talking about antiquities. I'm as interested in them in a casual way as you are, and when he said there were the foundations of a Quito temple in Riobamba I replied exactly what he wanted to hear – that I'd have liked to see them if only it had been daylight.

'He was all set on showing me the temple anyway, and we marched off sedately after dinner with Doña Clara's blessing and a couple of cigars. I don't think she would have let him go so easily, but her woman's instinct – you know, the one they pride themselves is never wrong – told her that I didn't much want to go and that I'd soon lead the expedition back to the hotel and her. As a matter of fact I was thinking the same as her husband – that the night was young and that if there was anything to do in Riobamba we might as well do it.'

'But is there a temple?' I asked.

'I don't know. Things began to move too fast. I've thought about it once or twice since, but whenever I ride into Riobamba I'm marketing or seeing friends, and damned if I ever remember to find out.

'Don Anastasio had never been on the loose in Riobamba and didn't know the town. Well, you or I would have asked at the hotel desk, but the vice-president went straight to the best authority – and that was the mayor. We hired a car and drove to his home and were told that he'd gone to the movies with his wife. So off we drove to the slush palace, and Don Anastasio hauls out the manager.

' "Flash a notice on the screen," he says, "to inform the *alcalde* that the vice-president is outside and wishes to speak to him."

'The manager recognised Don Anastasio and didn't hesitate. We waited in the car for three minutes or so, and out jumped the mayor like a bull into the ring – wild-eyed and blinking and so fast you'd have thought the doorman had stuck a dart into his bottom. He believed there was a revolution on.

'Don Anastasio calmed the alcalde down, and let him have a full string of compliments. Then he said he wanted him for an hour on urgent business and that he'd better go in again and tell his wife not to wait.

'But the alcalde wasn't doing anything so easy. Not on your life! He was swelling with importance. He wrote a note to his wife, and told the manager to flash *that* on the screen. His stock was up. He'd have something to talk about for the rest of his life.

'We put him in the car and the vice-president explained that I was a distinguished Englishman just passing through the country, and that I'd said I hadn't seen any pretty women in Ecuador. He was sorry he hadn't met me in time to show me Quito, but here we were, still on the Altiplano, and what about it? Of course I protested politely, but the alcalde was hurt. I gathered he was quite prepared to ring the church bells, declare a fiesta and have a parade of beauty up and down the main street.

'Don Anastasio put it to him what we wanted was more discreet amusement than that. The alcalde thought for a bit, and then gave the chauffeur an address. It was his girl's. He didn't produce her and he didn't invite us in; he just sent her off in another car to visit some of her pals. Then he helped us buy a case of champagne, gave us the keys of his country cottage and said good-night. He could keep his mouth shut, that alcalde. He's a senator now. Don Anastasio saw to that.

'It was a pretty little house about half an hour out of town with a patio full of flowers and a big fireplace and everything we could want. We hadn't had time for more than a bottle before the alcalde's young woman drove up, dropped three of her girlfriends at the front door and ran away laughing to the car before we could get a glimpse of her.

'You can imagine the rest for yourself. We woke up . . .'

'I can't imagine it,' I said.

'Well, that's right. Perhaps you can't. Or rather you'd imagine something much better than they really were. For the fact is they were more Indian than white and very solid.

'You know how it is. These Spanish-Americans need women about before they'll really let themselves go. And Anastasio let himself go as if he hadn't seen a woman or a guitar or a glass of wine in the last ten years. Lord, what a show! And every time he did anything particularly outrageous he'd clap me on the back and wish to God there were more Englishmen like me. He said they ought to appoint me British Minister to Ecuador. That was when I was showing the girls a dance I learned in Swaziland.

'Well, when the case was nearly empty, I thought I'd lie down and have a sleep. The room was pretty hot. I remember dreaming I was an orchid on the coast of Esmeralda, and the rain was making me grow into a fine, feeling, embracing sort of vegetable. I lay awake for a second or two, and, damn it, it *was* raining – at least I thought it was. What was really happening was that one of the girls was watering me with a watering-can. She was a gentle little creature. She couldn't bring herself to chuck the lot over my head.

'I squirted the last bottle of champagne at her, for I was feeling fine and thought she'd woken me up for purposes of her own. But then I saw that the chinks in the shutters weren't as black as they should have been. It was dawn and we hadn't more than half an hour to catch our train, if we had that. I made a dive for my watch, and saw we had thirty-five minutes.

'Anastasio was fast asleep on the floor with one girl's head on his knees and the other's on his chest. It was a pretty sight. I mean, a really pretty sight. There he lay with their black hair squandered all over his body, and looking like Jupiter asleep with his cupbearers. However, I hadn't time to go into that.

'I watered him a bit with the watering-can, and he sat up and laughed like hell.

' "*Jorge de mi alma!*" he shouts. "*El Ministro de la Gran*

Bretagna!" remembering his last joke as a man will when he wakes up with his liquor still on him, and the headache still an hour or two away.

'I pointed out that we had just thirty-two minutes to get to Riobamba station. I didn't mention Doña Clara. One shock was enough at a time.

' "Look for my clothes, Jorge," he said, "while I write a note to the alcalde."

'That was like him. He didn't know whether he'd see the man again, and he wasn't going without a word of thanks.

'I retrieved our clothes from the damned odd places they'd got to, and we put on whatever came to hand. Anastasio gave the girls a great wad of sucres, and we tumbled into the car. We did that run back to Riobamba in twenty minutes with no time to think of anything except sorting ourselves out. By the time we'd each got dressed in our own clothes we found we were only short one tie and one pair of socks. We tossed for them. He won the tie and I won the socks.

'There was Doña Clara in the hall of the hotel with all the baggage round her, and all the hotel staff and her team of porters trying not to laugh. You can imagine what we looked like. I can't answer for myself, but Anastasio had one of his moustaches up in the air and the other spread out flat like a wing. And his coat was all white with plaster where a bit of the ceiling had fallen on it.

' "*Queridita*," says Anastasio, "*queridita Clarita*, you will not believe me, but . . ."

'I tell you, I felt sorry. I've never seen such an angry woman. She'd been hurt, you see, right where it hurt most – in her pride. She might have forgiven him if nobody else had known that he'd stayed out all night. But here he was in front of all the people she'd been impressing for the last twelve hours.

' "*Se ha pasado algo muy raro*," Anastasio said.

'If you'd listened to the grave voice he put on you'd have believed what he said: that something very rare had come to pass. I knew he hadn't thought of what it was yet. But I could have sworn he was a just man to whom something outrageous had happened. Kidnapping or mistaken arrest.

' "*Muy raro*," he repeated, shaking his head. "*Muy raro*."

'Then he pretended to notice the time. He sent all those fellows running to the station, paid his bill, shot a man upstairs for my bag, and put on a tremendous show of activity which would keep him away from his wife until he could think of a story.

' "Jorge," he said to me, "for the love of God, what will I tell her?" and he giggled, for he was still in no state to see the awfulness of what had happened. 'You're the British Minister, Jorge,' he said to me. 'Think, *hijo mio*! Think of something!'

'Well, I was tight as a tick myself, and all I could think of was how damn funny he looked without any socks. And at that we went off into yells of laughter and staggered over to the station on the heels of Doña Clara.

The alcalde was there to see us off with some of the local worthies. Anastasio fell into his arms and began to thank him for the hospitality of Riobamba – but in such well-chosen words that nobody could tell exactly how much hospitality we had enjoyed. Then he introduced me all over again.

' "And let me tell you, *amigo*," he says to the alcalde, "that you have the honour of speaking to the new British Minister."

'The alcalde took him quite seriously, shook my hand and apologised for not having treated me with profounder respect the night before. The vice-president stared at him. Then he let out a whoop, linked his arms in the alcalde's and mine and led us at a run to the train. Thanks to the alcalde we got up the steps of the coach in good order and halted in front of Doña Clara. She looked clean through us, but that didn't stop Anastasio.

' "*Chiquita*," he says reproachfully, "why didn't you wait to hear what I was going to tell you? A triumph for us! A compliment! Our friend had a telegram last night appointing him British Minister to Ecuador – and who more fitted than Don Jorge? Are you surprised that we celebrated the good news, my angel? Isn't it natural that we should have drunk more than we should – and all the time wishing you had not been so tired so that you could have been with us!'

'She opened her mouth just long enough to say that she didn't believe a word of it. I smiled at her kindly and said that I should hardly jest about representing my country. She paid no attention to me.

'Then the alcalde tried his eloquence on her. He said that he was a married man himself and quite understood her feelings – and that he had been with us all the time to see that we came to no harm. He expressed his joy at being the first to greet the new Minister to Ecuador. Anybody could see, he said, that your humble servant was a person altogether out of the ordinary who had a long and honourable career before him. He was happy that friendship between the two great nations had reached the point when – and so on and so on. It filled the gap.

'Doña Clara asked where the telegram had been delivered, and Anastasio swore that I had been expecting it and called at the telegraph office to ask.

'Where is it?' she snapped.

' "Jorge," he said to me. "Where is it?"

'That beat me. I can't think at speed. I'm not a politician.

' "Mother of God!" said he. "You must have left it in the telegraph office when you sent the reply! Hold the train!" he ordered the station-master. "The British Minister has forgotten something!"

'We ran over to the telegraph office. Anastasio locked the door and had a few words with the operator. I'd not realised that to a vice-president all things are possible. Then he asked me the name of our Foreign Secretary. I didn't know. There was a Labour Government and I hadn't heard of any of them.

' "Look in your passport, chico!" he yelled.

'I looked. It was issued in 1922 and signed by Curzon. Those were the best passports we ever had. Old Curzon's jobs and titles filled a whole page. I tell you, those British passports used to impress the frontier police anywhere. After all, they're human like the rest of us.

'Anastasio pulled himself together and dictated the cable in Spanish. I put it into English – Clara could read English; she'd been educated in a high-class convent – and then that telegraph operator tapped it on his machine so that it came out printed on the tape. I've got it still.'

Trevithick opened his pocket-case and passed me a telegram, the creases of its folds finely pencilled by the accumulation of dust. It was quite faultless – stamped, dated, handed in at Quito and delivered at Riobamba, the strips of paper tape pasted on the usual form. It read:

TREVITHICK   RIOBAMBA
FOLLOWING CABLE RECEIVED FOR YOU FO CODE 37 DECODED HERE QUOTE BELIEVE ADVISABLE OPEN LEGATION QUITO WILL YOU ACCEPT APPOINTMENT HIS MAJESTYS MINISTER PLENIPOTENTIARY TO ECUADOR CABLE REPLY CURZON OF KEDLESTON UNQUOTE STOP HEARTY CONGRATULATIONS DO ACCEPT PENNYFATHER.

'Well, when we got back to the train we found that Doña Clara had been effecting repairs to her make-up – a sure sign that she was about half convinced. To help her over her embarrassment Anastasio showed her the cable, while I strolled up and down the platform followed by respectful stares and wishing I'd had time to shave. When they asked me if I would permit the train to leave I said I would, and climbed on board.

'Doña Clara was all over me with apologies. She had known from the start, she said, that my business in Quito was mysterious. She had expected something of this sort from the moment I got on the train. She knew it all along; she just knew it. It's odd how the stupider a woman is, the more she believes she has miraculous insight. Nature's compensation, I suppose. And then she asked me a lot of questions about the royal family, which I answered as best I could. I'm a monarchist every time, and they didn't suffer – but I did tell her she looked as if she had Bourbon blood herself. She was so flattered that when her husband pulled out a bottle of brandy that the alcalde had thoughtfully left with us, she just tapped him with her little gloves and told him he was a naughty Anastasio.

'We were a bit exhausted after all the hard thinking, and that brandy splashed into the remains of the champagne and set it working as if we'd just started on the night before. We were great. Great. Somebody must have sent word down the line that the new British Minister and the vice-president were on board, and at each little station there was a crowd to welcome us. I've never travelled in such state. They filled all the empty spaces in the coach with fruit and flowers and we made speeches from the observation platform and kissed their children, and every now and then the conductor would come down the train to ask if there was anything we wanted.

'Well, our mood went with the contour line. While we were climbing up to the last pass at twelve thousand feet, nothing could hold us. And we swooped over the edge of the Andes with the vice-president and the British Minister dancing on the observation platform, and half a dozen toy balloons – or what looked like them – tied to the rail and blowing out behind.

'When we had got down to five thousand, and stopped for lunch, I began to remember I wasn't the British Minister at all, but we had some more champagne at lunch and it kept us going. I stroked Doña Clara's hand and filled up my notebook with lunch and dinner engagements for the four days we should have to wait in Guayaquil before the boat left. I gathered that half a dozen of Clara's intimate friends were going north with us too, and she made me promise I'd be particularly polite to them on board. I let her think I was going back to London to settle my affairs before taking up the new post. As a matter of fact I was booked to Panama, and hadn't the faintest idea what I'd do when I got there.

'At sea level we cleaned ourselves up and slept for a bit. It was hot as hell. We were running through nigger villages and cocoa and banana plantations, and the sweat was rolling off us so thick that if you'd put a match to it, it would have lit. When we woke up we bought a couple of pineapples off

136

a little yellow girl and ate them and felt better. But the better we felt, the worse it was. I had nothing to lose myself, but by this time I loved Anastasio like a brother and I saw trouble ahead.

'At last he asked straight out what the hell we were to do now. We had both been thinking that on and off since lunch, but it was all right so long as neither of us said it. We could keep going if you see what I mean.

'I said I didn't know what we were to do – that the best thing would be for me to disappear as soon as we reached Guayaquil. Anastasio started to jump up and down. The heat was getting on his nerves. He said it wouldn't solve anything if I just vanished.

' "*Muy bien!*" I replied. "But you'll have to explain some time."

' "I won't!" he said. "I can't! Jorge" – he took my hand between two of his and fondled it just as I'd been doing to Doña Clara – "for the love of God, don't let me down!"

'Of course you can't realise what a stew we were in. You haven't met Doña Clara. Look at that picture! A self-important snob of a woman who would never let him forget that he'd once made a fool of her – let alone that fact that he'd come home without his socks. And the worst of it was that she was damned lovely. It just meant that if he confessed she'd have a double hold on him for the rest of his life.

'I said I'd do anything he liked – fall ill for the next four days in Guayaquil and miss the boat. But no – he wouldn't have it. I'd have the best doctors in Guayaquil and Clara at my bedside with a nurse's uniform and a big red cross on her shapely bosom. She wouldn't miss such a chance to be noble.

'Well, by now we were halfway across the marshes, running into Duran where you take the ferry for Guayaquil, and Doña Clara was trying on her picture hat. Before we'd had time to decide anything we were in Duran station, and a dozen of Clara's friends and Anastasio's politicos were there to meet us. He had to introduce me as the future British Minister, and that was that. We crossed the river to

Guayaquil in the President's private launch, and I was popular with the politicos, though I say so myself. The fact is, I think I missed my career. If a man can represent his country well when he's suffering from an evil conscience and a hangover he ought to be pretty damned good on a plain working day.

'We all pleaded tiredness after the journey, and except for a short reception at their house I didn't have to act any longer. Of course Clara wouldn't let me go to a hotel but insisted on putting me up. They had a house at Guayaquil as well as Quito and God knows where else. I went to bed at eight and slept like a log and didn't wake up till five in the morning, when I found Anastasio sitting by my bedside with a coffee-pot and some fruit-salts and the air of a family doctor watching his patient come round from the anaesthetic.

'He had that light in his eye. Quiet triumph, but a little unsure how I would react. Of course I asked him if he'd thought of anything. He shook his head and said he had, but that I wouldn't like it. Then he addressed me as earnestly as if I'd been leading the opposition in the senate. He put the problem very neatly: (a) I couldn't wait for the boat. If I did I should be entertained by all Guayaquil, and the President and Pennyfather would get to hear of it; (b) I couldn't just vanish, or Clara would smell a rat. So that we were left with (c) – that I must cease to be the British Minister openly and for good and sufficient reasons.

'Well, that was all right, given the reasons.

' "Did you ever take a bribe, Jorge?" he asked.

' "Not from a friend," I told him – and that was true.

' "Well, you have to take one from me," he went on, "and report to your government that it's not worth while to open a legation at Quito, and you won't accept the post.'

'I saw what he was after, but I couldn't see how it would help. True enough, he could say that for political reasons he didn't want a British Legation at Quito, and that he had bribed me to report against it and that I'd cleared out at once. But it didn't help. He could say it – but there was no proof of the bribe and no proof of the story. It wouldn't deceive a child, let alone Doña Clara.

'Still, the idea had possibilities, and I sat up in bed and considered them over the coffee. And then I saw how we could get out of the jam – he with honour and I with profit.

'I told him that the wisest thing was for me to take a bribe that everyone could see, and not to run away. Then he could tell his story and stand a chance of being believed.

' "Give me land," I said to him straight. "I like your country and you and your friends. I'll stay here. I'll keep my mouth shut. And this is what will happen. Doña Clara will believe you, and so will Riobamba. Pennyfather and your own foreign ministry will say that there was never any proposal to appoint a British Minister and that the whole rumour is ridiculous – which is just what they'd have to say if it were true. And they won't sound convincing, because there's me and my land to prove that you paid a good price for something – if it wasn't for refusing the British Legation, what was it for?"

'I felt a bit ashamed, for it sounded like blackmail. And in a way it was. Only I knew he wouldn't take it so. And I meant just a house and a few acres. I never expected all this.'

Trevithick waved his hand apologetically around the polished beauties of the dining-room.

'But Anastasio was wild with gratitude. It's funny, but do you know I think he was complimented that I wanted to live in his country – quite apart from the fact that I'd shown him the way out of the mess. He threw a dressing-gown at me and ran me down to the library, where he pulled out all his deeds and maps and photographs. I tell you, he might have conquered the country himself, he was so generous with it.

'What he offered at first wasn't what I wanted. He kept on insisting on coffee and cocoa and quinine and all the things I could grow that would make me rich. I told him that I was sick of trying to make money, that I wanted to settle down. Then he showed me this place. I could see it was pretty much what I had dreamed of, but too big. I hadn't any capital, I couldn't stock it.

' "I'll make you a sporting offer, Jorge," he said. "Take the place as it stands. It'll feed you and your men and keep a roof over your heads. And if you can't make that estancia pay its own running expenses, then you're an *hijo de puta* who ought to live in the same back street as your mother.

'I was short with him after that insult. I told him I'd forgotten more about grass farming than he ever knew, and I accepted the place. At nine o'clock he took me down to his lawyers and made out a deed of gift then and there – everything on the land moveable and immoveable as they say. I couldn't know it included this furniture and a volcano and the beginnings of the best dairy herd in Ecuador, could I?'

'No,' I answered. 'But what did people say?'

'Exactly what I prophesied. And I called the ranch "La Embajada" to encourage them a bit. And those who didn't believe our story started a rumour that Anastasio had bought me off because he didn't dare let me travel on the same boat with his wife. So I had her portrait painted and hung it up to let them have a bit of evidence on their side as well. Of course that was long ago. I think everybody knows the real truth now – except Doña Clara.'

No Police in the Cemetery

The return of the Conde de Villanueva to his ancestral home had not been as gay and pleasurable as he expected. In his little town of Lazalaya, in the sun-striped Café Moderno to which he had looked forward through months of darkened New York bars, even in the office of the mayor who had always treated him with a fatherly affection in which there was no room for formal respect, he had been received with cold courtesy. Added to that, there was upon his desk a note from the Civil Governor of the Province demanding his immediate presence.

He really couldn't blame them. The price offered by a Hamburg tourist agency for a strip of his foreshore had so pleasantly surprised him that he cabled his acceptance and signed the documents without remembering his own romantic view of geography. His education had left him permanently muddled between the points of the compass. Eagerly following in his school books the westward track of the conquistadores, the Pacific, the Philippines and even India appeared to him obviously west of Spain, the world east of Spain stopping somewhere about the Persian Gulf. His mental block was a mere question of semantics and impossible to refute; but on the dry land of a surveyor it was a nuisance, a disease, a curse. He believed that he had sold the eastern headland when he had actually sold the western.

The mistake hurt his pride – not his ancestral pride which hardly existed, but his self-respect as an enterprising young businessman with a taste for public relations. And he was appalled to find how irrevocably his error had grown. The foundations of a luxury hotel and the terracing of the approach road were already recognisable on the headland.

The walls of a single-storied service wing – staff quarters, laundry, store-rooms and garage – were awaiting the roof. Bustling about the whole disaster with Teutonic efficiency was the able Herr Carl Kuchler who had chosen the site and would be ready within a year to receive the hotel coaches full of citron-blooming compatriots impatient to toast their white navels and patronise the Mediterranean.

On his third day home Gil de Villanueva obeyed the summons of the Civil Governor. Official displeasure was easier to face than all those unofficial silences. He drove to the provincial capital and parked his car with a final cavalier gesture in the space reserved for the Governor himself.

The Palace restored his faith in himself and his society. It was entirely unfitted for the enlightened, modern administration of a province. The Ministry of the Interior wished, he knew, to build a glass-and-concrete block of government offices, whereupon the Ministry of Tourism, always eager to turn the useless and beautiful into a superb hotel, would have gladly taken over the Palace. But nobody – thank God! – had yet had the heart to change its traditional function.

This treasure of Spanish baroque, its crumbling yellow stone combining elegance with power, had even affected the Governor's appearance. The distinguished twentieth-century lawyer, who had never been gravely disturbed if some remains of his lunch were visible on his waistcoat in the afternoon, was now all courtly and fastidious. He wore the same perfectly cut black suits that he had always worn, but he treated the cloth as if it were lace and black velvet. He had suppressed the grey-and-black moustache which gave him a certain air of authority in the clubs and cafés of Madrid, and now showed an austere and scholarly upper lip. When he was annoyed – and at the moment he was very annoyed indeed – the lip was as long as if it had been painted by El Greco.

He frowned upon the young man, the far too self-satisfied young man, sitting opposite his tremendous desk of olive wood and mahogany. Both were dwarfed by the sheer space of the Governor's office and its lofty stone walls hung with tapestries and pictures, some of them in place since the reign of Philip III, some lent by the paternal State.

'As a grandee of Spain you ought to be ashamed of yourself!' Don Baltasar announced. 'Because of your continued absence from your estates, irresponsible attorneys have been able to sell to a speculator the land promised by your father to the Municipality of Lazalaya.'

'Nobody could regret it more than I do, Excellency. If your colleagues of the Law – excuse me, your former colleagues – could ever draw up a conveyance making it clear exactly what one is selling, it wouldn't have happened.'

The Count appeared completely unimpressed by his surroundings. The casual air of good breeding, which he could no more help than his distinctively Spanish narrow face and slim physique, contained neither disrespect nor undue reverence. He was in fact thinking that the grave magnificence framing Don Baltasar would have suited his own tastes and appearance a great deal better; it was a pity that he could not consider the arts of government as anything but a joke.

'I am prepared to grant that under the influence of feminine and other distractions you did not read the conveyance with due care,' said the Civil Governor severely. 'But what you have done is to allow a lousy German tourist agent to put up a hotel where the Municipality proposed to build a mole and a fish market whenever they could raise the capital. You, the Conde de Villanueva, have broken a contract!'

'There was nothing in writing, was there?'

'In dealing with your father it was not necessary to put anything in writing. And he was not, I will again impress on you, an absentee landlord.'

'Your Excellency talks as if we still owned half the province instead of just a farm at Lazalaya.'

'The principle is the same.'

'With respect, it is not the same. My father fed and educated his family by running a small estate with extreme efficiency. Myself I am a disaster as a farmer. So I leave the management to a bailiff and meanwhile sell sherry in New

York, thereby adding to the country's exports. And I refuse to be called an absentee landlord,' Gil went on, adding a calculated warmth to his defence. 'If I am, why don't you people expropriate me? Exactly! Because it isn't worth the trouble for four hundred hectares of land upon which, I may point out, the labourers are known to be well paid, happy, well-housed – and no monkey business with the social security. I also remind you that on my last visit I was publicly congratulated by the local Syndicate of Agricultural Workers.'

'They were all as drunk as owls,' replied the Civil Governor, 'and so were you.'

'The ancient democracy of Spain . . .'

'I can do without a lecture on politics. The point is you sold it.'

'Your Excellency should not have allowed it.'

'I wasn't asked. It all went through the Ministry of Tourism.'

'Lack of liaison, I shall complain to the Chief of State through my Syndicate.'

'You haven't got a Syndicate.'

'I have. Employees of the Wine Industry. And if it hasn't enough nuisance value, I'll stand for the Municipality of Lazalaya. I'm sure to be elected, however much you try to cook the returns.'

'I do not cook the returns.'

'And your Excellency will find himself governing Guinea with only two retired generals for company.'

'I tell you I never had a chance to intervene,' Don Baltasar insisted, picking up a symbolic file and slapping it with his other hand.

'I accept your word. I am glad you have the decency to apologise.'

'It is not an apology.'

'Well, it sounded like one. Am I, once and for all, an absentee landlord?'

'In spirit, no.'

'That will do, Excellency. I am now prepared to help.'

'I wish you would stop calling me Excellency.'

'You started it, my dear uncle, by addressing me as Conde de Villanueva. The least I expected was exile and a fine.'

'You know very well, Gil, that my powers are limited.'

'To whatever you can get away with. Why don't you compel this Kuchler to sell the land back to the Municipality?'

'Because I can't and should be sacked if I tried. I must remind you that it is deliberate Government Policy, executed in practice by the Ministry of Tourism, to turn Spain into a holiday camp for all Europe. Foreign Exchange, the Family, Employment . . .'

'I don't see all the males of Lazalaya becoming waiters.'

'Nor do I! Nor do I!' said the Civil Governor, making the considerable circuit of his desk and putting an arm round the shoulders of his nephew. 'All I can suggest is that you show a sense of responsibility in future, and by active cooperation with your decent fellow citizens endeavour to revive in them some respect for the family. I need not say that I am entirely at the disposition of the Municipality of Lazalaya.'

Gil de Villanueva drove slowly back along the excellent road which was – economically speaking – the cause of all the trouble. It had been built by his grandfather in the days of family prosperity, and for a long generation had been used only by mule carts and the Villanueva automobile. Lazalaya had never had any reason for existence except that it existed.

The road and the rapid increase of fast and efficient transport had at least suggested that the town ought to be originating traffic rather than receiving it at a dead end. Fish was the answer – an imaginative answer, since Lazalaya had always ignored the sea. The coast was grim and rocky without a sheltered anchorage. Still, only two miles away, there was a shallow cove where a small and active community of inshore fishermen worked their rowing boats from a semicircular beach and supplied by donkey and pack basket the town and its surrounding villages. Given a breakwater of a hundred metres to protect the cove from the prevailing south-easterly winds, Lazalaya could become the only fishing port on a long, inhospitable shore.

Civil War had prevented the development; then lack of capital. Neither Lazalaya or the Villanuevas had any money. The central and provincial governments were fully occupied by more essential schemes. Meanwhile the road had attracted Herr Kuchler and a few adventurous tourists – at any rate to the extent that it was now safer to ride a donkey on the right rather than down the middle.

Gil de Villanueva stopped and got out on the crest of the low range which separated the narrow coastal plain from the endless inland miles of scrub and poor cornland. In his own territory he felt a car to be a confinement of the spirit; he preferred the old-fashioned view from the back of a horse.

Below him to his right – west, damn it! – was the compact little town, its lack of any brick or concrete suburbs revealing that it had not the least excuse for growth. To his left was the great, green oblong of the Villanueva farm, separated from the prevailing yellows of the countryside by a plastered stone wall – an extravagantly expensive method of fencing which dated from the time when labour cost little. The fertility within the wall reminded him of his father who had created it. And that unpleasantly emphasized what his father would have thought of him.

A remarkable vehicle was pounding unconcernedly up the hairpin bends of the road. The front of it was a twin-engined motorcycle with its handlebars enclosed in a cabin; the back was that of a small van. It belonged to the mayor, and had indeed been built by him in his own workshop. Since he was the smith, coachbuilder and wheelwright of Lazalaya and described himself as Engineer, it was a striking advertisement for his crafts. Forged iron and sound timber made it indestructible, and on such a hill would probably have made it immoveable if not for an additional gear of three massive cogs and shafts. Even so, the steady climbing was mysterious, for the home-made first gear must have weighed nearly as much as the engine.

Gil's first instinct was to turn round and escape the meeting. He was humiliated to think that the mayor might not even stop to talk. But such cowardice would not do,

146

really would not do. So he placed his own car more or less in the middle of the road, and himself posed sadly and romantically upon a roadside rock.

Don Jaime Caruncho halted his shuddering chimera, and at least exchanged compliments.

'And what are you thinking about up there?' he asked. 'Lunch?'

'Far from it, Jaime. I am recovering from an interview with the Civil Governor.'

'What was His Excellency's opinion?'

'Of me?'

'That I can guess. Of what should be done.'

'Civil Governors, my dear Jaime, only think what they think they ought to think. That is why they are appointed. All I can tell you is that he would rather have fish than a hotel.'

'Are you sure of that?'

'Of course. He drew himself up to his full width and ordered me to cooperate with decent people.'

'Then I will try to find a use for you.'

'Anything you like,' said Gil, joining the mayor in the road and absent-mindedly patting the vehicle. 'Where are you going?'

'To buy a second-hand dynamo.'

'Second-hand dynamos don't work.'

'They do when I have repaired them.'

'If I were to accompany you in the back of the van . . .'

'No. For the time being we should continue to appear on the worst possible terms.'

'How right you are, Jaime! The strength of you natural leaders is in the instinctive reactions which allow you time to think.'

'Enough compliments! Do you agree with us that this hotel will be a disaster for the morale of Lazalaya?'

Gil did not. He thought that both the influence and the economic effects of the hotel would be excellent. But what mattered was the site for the long-promised breakwater.

'Jaime, I always accept expert opinion,' he answered

cautiously. 'This Kuchler, however, is a heretic and will not.'

'He must answer to God for it. Meanwhile you can ask him to dinner.'

'What do you want me to say?'

'Nothing! Nothing! Just to look mysterious if he asks your opinion on some curiosities that I have told him. He is very interested in the atrocious past of Lazalaya, and it seems to me that he is too sure of the future. Some of those exaggerations you loose off when you have been drinking would do no harm.'

'Anything else?'

'We will see how it goes. Well, I'm off. On your way back take a look at the house in the Travesía de San Bartolomeo where Kuchler is staying. Something may occur to you.'

When he reached Lazalaya, Gil walked slowly through the Travesia. Nothing whatever occurred to him, except that Jaime would never take action without the approval of his friends, the priests. He was a conservative of conservatives, an ardent and practising churchman and above suspicion. Reliability without speed. The Vehicle was a true expression of his character – though it might be as well to remember that within his workshop Jaime was ruthless with his materials.

The Travesía was a long, narrow alley behind the Church, with half-abandoned warehouses on one side and a high wall, which had once enclosed a nunnery, on the other. The only two houses were Father Miguel's, next to the church, and a venerable, crumbling mansion nearly opposite, of which Herr Kuchler had taken the second floor. The alley was private enough for anything, even for Kuchler's assassination – though that could hardly have entered into the calculations of Jaime and the *cofradía* of the Friends of San Bartolomeo who probably represented as well as anyone the 'decent people' referred to by his uncle. Feeling more obscured by ecclesiastical shadows than an experienced Villanueva ought to feel, he dropped a note to Kuchler asking him to dinner the following day.

As yet he had only talked to the speculator at the hotel site or on the beach, reluctant to join him in the Café Moderno and be received by its customers with an elaborate politeness which really hurt. Kuchler, no doubt, would have ascribed it to respect for an ancient family. In his determination not to put a foot wrong in Spain he took social rank too seriously. That was the only reason why Gil had not already offered hospitality; Kuchler would be disappointed that it was so easily come by.

The German was extremely presentable, arriving with his white dinner jacket and formal air. A well-preserved man in his late forties with china-blue eyes in a smooth face of even tan, he was straight off the cover of a magazine for elder citizens – if there was such a thing. He turned out to be a likeable guest, and would have been even more so if he had not been so anxious to be liked.

Passion was the only word for Kuchler's admiration of Spain and its people. Gil was reminded of an unfortunate friend of his who had been determined to marry a gipsy singer and was always making excuses or denying that any need for excuses existed. He suspected that Kuchler knew the country chiefly from books, though speaking excellent Castilian. He was too slow to appreciate the dancing of light and shade.

'I hope, Count, that you are content with our deal?' Kuchler asked at last.

'Very, my dear fellow, very! When I think of the bare . . .'

'And I intend to pay particular attention to the restaurant.'

'The little bikinis!' Gil exclaimed.

'Ha! Ha!'

'And the intriguing possibilities of my house!'

'You will invite me. I hope.'

'Of course! Of course!' Gil replied, and then remembered that he was under orders.

The revolutionary past of Lazalaya had not been notably atrocious, except in Jaime's eyes. Still, over the years there had been quite enough incidents for brandy and imagination to work on.

'If I can,' he added. 'It is such a pity that for us the sincerity of political opinions can only be proved by violence.'

'But all is very calm,' Kuchler insisted. 'In the north and in the universities I know there are pockets of discontent. But here is old Spain! The true, old, catholic Spain!'

'Yes, we haven't changed much.'

'So wonderful in our era! So uniquely restful!'

'And always so predictable. Do you know that this house has been burnt down four times since 1800?'

'But by whom?' Kuchler asked, much shocked.

'Usually Lazalaya. We deserved what was coming to us except the accompanying rape,' said Gil, warming to his task. 'And my father used to tell me that from what he remembered of his great-aunts they deserved that, too.'

'But rape!'

'We can always have bikinis prohibited. That won't keep people away if the food is good enough.'

'Surely Lazalaya does not object to the hotel?' Kuchler asked. 'There was, I believe, some project for a mole.'

'Oh, that! They've been talking about that since 1930. Your hotel will make more money for them than sardines. And prosperity for everyone is bound to reduce the crime statistics.'

'There is no crime! My partner and I consulted our Embassy and the provincial chief of security.'

Gil had to admit that there were very few arrests. He tried to make his tone regretful. Herr Kuchler fidgeted with his bow tie and finished his brandy with a decisive gulp.

'I was talking to Don Jaime Caruncho a few days ago,' he said. 'He asked me if I had ever visited the cemetery.'

'And have you?'

'Casually. In passing. And then he put a most curious question: had I ever noticed that no police were buried there?'

'Oh, I see.'

'He seemed unwilling to tell me any more, and suggested that I should ask you.'

'Ask me what?' Gil replied, his mind racing for some answer which would satisfy Jaime and yet be noncommittal.

'Why there are no police in the cemetery.'

'Well, they aren't buried there.'

'Where are they buried?'

'Who knows, my dear Carl, who knows? I will ask you a question in my turn. Have you ever seen a dead donkey?'

'No. No, I don't believe I have.'

'Think it over! You are an intelligent man.'

Kuchler's thanks were impenetrable. When he got into his car to drive back to Lazalaya, he certainly seemed graver than he should have been after a Villanueva dinner; but Gil doubted if this able and active German was likely to be still impressed at breakfast time in the Travesía de San Bartolomeo. Jaime Caruncho's dark hints were childish.

He strolled with a last cigar on the terrace of his house. Faint specks of lanterns showed at sea where the little boats had their lines out for bream. Lazalaya was a soft pattern of light, composed of faint pools rather than bright points. The only intrusion of modernity was the sudden plunge of a newly bought heifer as her nose touched the electric fence which limited the dairy herd's supper of lucerne.

Gil's peace of mind, already insecure between amusement and misgivings, had barely recovered from the start when there was a second plunge from the pomegranate grove below him.

'How did it go?' asked the mayor.

'Jaime, I wish you would arrive by the front door. And such impatience is undignified.'

'We technicians have no time for dignity.'

'But for a little refreshment, I hope.'

'Here outside the house, if you like.'

Gil, returning from the dining-room with glasses and a bottle, determined to reimpose his authority. It was futile for Lazalaya, a town of four thousand inhabitants without any noticeable capital among the lot, to oppose a sound

151

project conceived in Hamburg and approved by the Ministry
of Tourism.

'Look, old friend! Forgive me if I say that you do not
know the world outside Spain! When a speculator such as
Kuchler has made so large an investment, he is not easily
frightened out of it – if, as I suspect, that's your intention.'

'We will see. Tell me – what are his politics?'

'He seems to be much like an American. He gives political
names to his decency and good will, and has no interest in
definition.'

'But it is said he was a Nazi,' Jaime replied.

'Almost inevitable in a man of his age.'

'Well, it counts. He was brought up to violence.'

'So were you,' Gil retorted, for the mayor had been a
twice-decorated sergeant-major in the crusade against the
infidel Republic.

'That is why I understand him. He has a natural distrust
of the Left.'

'Jaime, you are not to involve them! They'd go to gaol.'

'What do you think of me?' the major exclaimed indignantly. 'Whatever their misguided past, they are now my
fellow citizens. I shall ensure that they all have alibis.'

'When? What for?'

'Father Miguel will explain to you. Go and see him
tomorrow.'

Ridiculous, but at least harmless, Gil thought as he rode
into Lazalaya the following day. His only touch of aristocratic pride was in his attitude to the Church. Since it was
essential to the State, it must always be able to count on
Villanueva support. As for parish priests, one entertained
them; one had profound respect for their office; but one
was not bound to have any for their opinion.

Father Miguel always reminded him of an obscure traffic
signal. His cheek-bones were red, and so was the tip of his
pointed nose. They formed a triangle under the black line
of his eyebrows. He was cordial enough – and he damned
well should be – but the parochial chair was uncomfortable
and the interview unsatisfactory. Jaime seemed to have been
misinformed, or else Father Miguel's system of approach

bidding was very cautious. He was pretending to see no harm in the hotel.

'I fear it is likely to bring in disturbing modern influence, padre,' Gil remarked gravely.

'That is nothing new for the church, my son.'

'Well, no. Of course not. Still, I can imagine . . .'

'Sometimes fact is more healthy than imagination.'

'I was only thinking that if we are to make out a case . . .'

'The Ministry of Tourism has the full approval of the Church. It is not for me, a humble parish priest, to question national policy.'

'But I understand you would rather have an honest little port and a fish-market! What about St Peter?'

'I cannot feel that he would have objected to a well-run inn.'

'Roman orgies, padre?'

'I am unable to decide how much you hope, my son, and how much you fear. So far as I know, the hotel will be primarily for respectable families from northern Europe.'

This was getting nowhere. It was hardly worthwhile bringing up the question of female exposure. The old fox was quite capable of pointing out that nothing was more likely to impress on Lazalaya the vanity of the flesh than respectable wives in bikinis.

'I can well see that you wish to undo the results of a moment of carelessness,' Father Miguel went on. 'But even if this worthy Kuchler could be persuaded to abandon the project, even if you were able to repay him his money, which – forgive me if I am misinformed – you cannot do, how is the Municipality to raise the capital for a mole and a fishmarket?'

'Well, we could always try the banks or float a company. We should have the foundations. That's an asset. And since the fishmarket would not be so big as the hotel, we can sell what's over.'

'To whom?'

'A canning factory, for example.'

'There is not enough space.'

'Well, a villa then.'

'Would you wish to live on top of a fishmarket?'

'You're being very difficult, padre.'

'I am perhaps inexperienced, my son. And has it occurred to you that the walls of the service wing are three metres high already? Your company would have all the expense of pulling them down, and I doubt if the Ministry of Tourism would allow it. Our little town is powerless to oppose the Government.'

'I told Jaime that.'

'If only the site were in the centre of a business district!' Father Miguel rambled on. 'I hear that a constructor of office buildings has made an offer to the Little Brothers of St Macario for their convent in Tarragona. The price will enable them very materially to extend their good works.'

'Then they had better take it,' said Gil impatiently.

He was exasperated. It was typical of these parish priests to take refuge in milk-and-vinegar neutralism and start blathering about Little Brothers.

'They would indeed if they could find a simple priory. The roof they would build with their own hands.'

'I'd suggest some fairly heavy gloves.'

'It would be well within their capacities to complete the service wing. In California, I am told, missions are turned into hotels. I see no reason why here we should not turn a hotel into a mission.'

'And a lot of use that would be to Lazalaya! I mean, no doubt the town would profit spiritually, but . . .'

'If the Little Brothers had the hotel garden and the wing,' replied Father Miguel gently, 'I cannot believe they would object to the excellent investment of building and owning a fishmarket. That leaves us only with the problem of financing the mole. No doubt the Little Brothers would assist, especially if the Provincial Government, under its present enlightened administration, were to give a grant.'

'It's possible. But something on paper . . .' Gil began.

'Indeed something on paper! With a little compass, perhaps, on the map? For example: that if for any unknown cause the building of the hotel is abandoned and the site with existing improvements offered back to you, the Little

154

Brothers would lend you the money, you on your part giving them a lien on the property at cost, and they on their part undertaking to build a fishmarket with all necessary approaches and customary amenities and to lease the same to the Municipality on condition that the Municipality, whom I believe we should call the Party of the Third Part, undertake to build a mole and a quay.'

For a moment Gil could find no reply, feeling that astonishment at the extreme competence of the Church would be rude and congratulations out of place. Eventually he mumbled that they would have to keep the deal pretty quiet.

'Publicity is always to be deprecated, my son. You may count, I assure you, on the discretion of the legal advisers to the Church. Now, since you appear to agree, let me hear your proposal, always remembering that I cannot run very fast.'

'Padre, I have no proposal whatever!'

'I understand from Don Jaime that you suggest I should allow a party of revolutionaries to chase me down the Travesía.'

'I know absolutely nothing about it,' Gil protested excitably.

'Let me put your conscience at rest! I see no sacrilege in so good a cause, especially since this regrettable scene will be organised by the Cofradía of San Bartolomeo. All that will be asked of you personally is to keep your uncle informed – without in any way compromising him of course – so that in case of need he may, as the saying is, hold the ring.'

'He'll shove me up before a military court if he thinks I'm responsible!'

'Surely not! Surely not! He will rejoice that a grandee of Spain should stick at nothing to undo the results of an accidental breach of faith. And in any case the Little Brothers will see that the Bishop has a word with him. God be with you, my worthy son!'

Back in the calm of the far too empty ancestral home, Gil realised that if anything went wrong the sacrifice had been already chosen. The scapegoat would be the irresponsible young man who had sold the headland, who didn't go to church if he could help it, who approved of impropriety on beaches, who could buy an air passage one jump ahead of the police. There was no way out but ignominious flight. And that wouldn't do at all. Some time in the future – when a rich wife came along or America doubled its consumption of sherry – Lazalaya would again be his permanent home; and home, if it meant anything, meant the liking and trust of his fellow citizens from top to bottom.

In the evening the Vehicle rumbled openly up the drive to the house. That at least was a welcome sign.

'I thought we had agreed to keep our distance,' said Gil cautiously, after he had led the mayor into his study and shut the door.

'That doesn't matter any longer now that all the decent people know you are doing your best.'

'Well, you can go straight back and tell them that I will not chase Father Miguel down the Travesía de San Bartolomeo.'

'Nothing of that for you! All that's needed is for you to be with Kuchler in his dining-room which overlooks the street. Have you got a pistol?'

'No and no! And I don't want one.'

'Well, take this!' said the mayor, handing over a neat Star automatic.

'What for?'

'Just to take a few shots at us when we pass Kuchler's flat.'

'I might easily hit you.'

'What about all the prizes you won for pigeon shooting?'

'One does not use a pistol,' Gil shouted.

'The principle is the same.'

'Kuchler will get suspicious.'

'On the contrary! He will be convinced. You are an excitable young man of good family defending the Church. It is not necessary to know the difference between east and west at short range.'

'Anything else?' Gil asked, accepting his fate.

'Yes. It's fixed for the seventeenth.'

'Why?'

'No moon. And I can arrange for Alonso Mejias and Enrique Jimenez to be on duty at the bottom of the Travesía.'

'Can't you find someone more intelligent?' Gil asked, for the two venerable constables had piously dreamed their way through thirty years of Lazalaya's civic and ecclesiastical life. 'They are just a pair of unfortunates.'

'That is because their minds are not set on things of this world, Gil,' said the mayor rebukingly. 'They see nothing. They are still incapable of holding up a bicycle with one hand while beckoning on my Vehicle with the other.'

'Suppose Kuchler can't have me to dinner on the seventeeth?'

'Of course he can! What has he to do except walk round his headland learning filthy language from the builders? Good! And try to look more cheerful in public!'

By enlisting the aid of Kuchler's venerable cook who had learned her job in the Villanueva kitchens, Gil managed to force the invitation with complete naturalness. She had only to mention that a dish of sea bream, stuffed with garlic, had been a favourite of the *señorito*. Kuchler, bored by his usually lonely meals, was on the telephone at once and accepted the date of the seventeenth. A more formal dinner, he said, must come later, and meanwhile this would be a memorable occasion.

Memorable it certainly was. Gil tried hard to be a satisfactory guest, though feverishly mopping up his sauce, talking too fast and probably drinking too much. The more he looked at the repercussions of this scandal, the more nervous he was. Everyone else was safe. The veterans of the republican army, the former anarchists, communists and plain democrats, were all sitting comfortably in their accustomed Café Ventura under the eyes of the town. The members of the Cofradía of San Bartolomeo were above suspicion. Nobody would ever enquire where they were.

Gil surreptitiously watched the ancient wall-clock behind Kuchler's head. It formally struck eleven at ten minutes to the hour. His own watch said it was five past. But the time told by Jaime's immense pocket watch, mended and improved by himself, was the only time of importance. He wondered how in the Civil War Spaniards ever managed to synchronise an attack. Whose watch? What check on it? And then at last came the flash and the formidable explosion.

'What the devil was that?' Kuchler exclaimed, rushing to the window.

Gil nearly answered that it was sugar and weed-killer. He hadn't believed it could possibly be so effective. But trust Jaime! He probably used it for testing the springs of the Vehicle.

Father Miguel shot out of the vestry door and down the Travesía, shouting for help. Simultaneously the north end of the church glowed red behind the high wall as a pile of paraffin-soaked rafters from the former nunnery flared and crackled.

Hot on the heels of Father Miguel raced six men, collars turned up, faces indistinguishable in the darkness. Gil threw open the window, drew his pistol and sprayed the nunnery wall, hoping that one shot at least had gone reasonably close to the figure which he took to be Jaime. The flying shadows were seen for a moment down the street against the glow of light from the plaza, and disappeared.

'The church is burning,' Kuchler shouted, rushing for the door. 'We must help.'

'I shouldn't if I were you. These things happen from time to time. One ignores them.'

'But you fired! A little high, if you permit an old soldier to say so.'

'I think I hit one. We keep the peace ourselves in Lazalaya. The honour of the town demands it.'

'Where are the police?'

'The police know better than to interfere, my dear Carl. I believe Don Jaime told you that . . . well . . . they sometimes disappear. May I perhaps have another brandy?'

The only thing which could appear suspicious to anyone who knew Lazalaya was the speed with which the fire engine arrived. Since Jaime Caruncho ran the Fire Brigade as well

as the town, that was not surprising. Near the far end of
the Travesía was a small turning to the left which led to
the fire station. The conspirators had evidently taken refuge
there. Those who were volunteer fire-fighters had then
dragged out the engine; those who were not had quietly
mixed with the excited crowd coming up from the plaza.
Father Miguel's discreet movements were beyond guessing.

'It is my duty to report what we saw,' Kuchler insisted.

'Just to the mayor, perhaps. We can trust him to be
discreet. Lazalaya does not want to lose the hotel.'

'They are going the right way to do it!' Kuchler exclaimed
indignantly. 'But of course, as one of yourselves, I know
that I must not take these little outbreaks too seriously.
Now shall I tell Don Jaime you fired?'

'So long as you don't tell anyone else. These people, you
understand, might visit me and turn out better shots than I
am.'

'But suppose, my dear Count, that they think it was I
who shot at them?'

'Oh, they wouldn't mind that! Just a German doing his
duty, they would say. They'd know there was no ill feeling
behind it.'

Kuchler next day upon his building site looked charged
with secrets, but there was nothing in that to draw attention
to him since all the citizens of Lazalaya were equally
distraught. Their animation was insistent, though expressed
in voices more muted than usual. Any person of some
education was as ashamed to be ignorant of what had
happened as any leader of a large community forced to
admit that he hadn't read the newspapers for a week. Inside
information, as a matter of prestige, had to be freely
invented.

Father Miguel, as befitted his cloth, did not tell a single
lie. He had heard an explosion, seen flames and run for
help. When it was discovered that nothing more than a pile
of old rafters had caught fire, he was much relieved. Shots?
No, he was quite sure that nobody had shot at him. Perhaps
people had heard the crackling of the fire. He was no scien-

tist, but could not all be explained by spontaneous combustion?

Don Jaime massively recommended calm; and the town police, who had not a clue to the culprits – for their only representatives anywhere near the spot had been Jimenez and Mejias – accepted his ingenious theory that the fire was a distasteful prank of students who considered, it might be, that Lazalaya needed waking up. Alternatively, idle foreigners from the vicious resorts along the coast might be responsible. The fishermen of the cove were persuaded that they had seen mysterious headlights racing up the hill from Lazalaya. The fire, the explosion and the shots, which the whole plaza had heard even if Father Miguel had not, were the only certain facts.

After a couple of days it was obvious that Kuchler's intentions were unaffected. He took the generous view that, though there might be occasional excitement in Lazalaya, the hotel was too far from it to be involved. Should tourists, as tourists do, sometimes wish to spend their money in the cafés of the town, he was quite sure that they would only be impressed by the unfailing courtesy of the Spaniard to the foreigner. He had some evidence, he said tactfully to Don Jaime, that Lazalaya could control its own affairs without interference, and undoubtedly, for the sake of the hotel, it would.

'He thinks we have declared our independence like Gibraltar,' the mayor announced to Gil. 'We have surpassed ourselves!'

'*You* have.'

'And who has been bombarding the town with a pistol? I was hit by a flake of plaster from the wall.'

'If you were, you wouldn't have known it with all those clothes round your head.'

'It was the size of a plate! Look, Gil – what we have to do now is to prove to Kuchler that the authorities take us seriously. The Governor's secretary is in my office.'

'What does he want?'

'You.'

'I'm busy. Tomorrow. Next week.'

160

'He has come to pick you up and drive you to the Palace. You have to go.'

'I warn you – I shall tell Don Baltasar the truth.'

'Nothing better!' Jaime replied cheerfully. 'He's on our side. You said so. Show some spirit, friend! We're still a long way from the fish market.'

Well, spirit was the only thing to show, plus some of the blackmail which had been applied to himself. Gil found his uncle in a pose of imperial neutrality, framed by the great room of power, and at once took the offensive.

'You look like Pontius Pilate,' he remarked.

'I would remind you that he had no difficulty in dealing with two thieves.'

'You have heard then that there has been a bomb in Lazalaya?'

'I have had fifteen security reports, each one more improbable than the last, and I begin to fear that our noble police, like those of other countries, create smoke in order to justify their salaries. I have sent for you to tell me what fire, if any, there really was.'

'A little one – in the old nunnery.'

'And you?' Don Baltasar stormed. 'You were concerned in this criminal folly?'

'Your Excellency told me to cooperate with my decent fellow citizens.'

'My only hope is that we can put it down to agitation by the Left.'

'No, you can't. Jaime Caruncho was very careful to see that they all had alibis.'

'Well, what the devil am I going to do if this comes to the ears of the Government?'

'Jaime will tell you what to do.'

'I am not going to have the mayor of a collection of insanitary hovels telling the Civil Governor what he is to do! And I remind you that Our Movement would have no objection to sending a grandee of Spain to gaol with a long sentence, and might even welcome the opportunity. I also remind you . . .'

'If you'd let me explain,' Gil interrupted.

'I do not wish to know the details. You can merely tell me this. What interest has the Bishop got in the fishmarket and the mole?'

'I suppose he disapproves of bikinis.'

'Nonsense!' Don Baltasar roared. 'He's a modernist. And he knows very well that if the Ministry of Tourism says there will be bikinis, bikinis there will be. Our need for Foreign Exchange . . .'

'The Little Brothers of St Macario also need a priory.'

'Would you do me the honour to amplify that statement? Concisely and with respect both for my intelligence and my office!'

Gil put forward Father Miguel's proposal as confidently as a real estate operator proposing to pyramid mortgages on a dubious title. The Civil Governor listened with growing calm, perceiving that he was not entirely isolated between the Cabinet and his irresponsible home town.

'I always understood the Little Brothers to be an Order of Poverty,' he said severely.

'Perhaps that is why they have some savings.'

'And I have no intention of holding the ring, as your Father Miguel puts it. You, Jaime Caruncho and the Cofradia of San Bartolomeo will be defenceless before the Ministry. So shall I. I propose to take immediate steps to cover myself and show that I am not a man to be trifled with.'

'I am sure that would be wise, uncle. As a matter of interest, how far do you control the Civil Guard?'

'Control is a strong word. I indicate my wishes to the Commanding Officer and he takes them into account.'

'Then may I suggest that you station a detachment in Lazalaya – just to restore confidence among foreigners?'

'It's the last thing which would restore confidence!'

'Your Excellency understands me perfectly.'

'It understands that you are an impertinent young crook! It also impresses on you that It cannot lift a finger to save you, since the Chief of State disapproves of nepotism and It has the misfortune to be your uncle.'

'We should only want them a few days. And tell them to behave themselves!'

'The discipline of the Civil Guard is impeccable.'

'I know it is. But they needn't look quite so grim.'

'What are they supposed to be there for?'

'To show the Ministry that you are not a man to be trifled with, my dear uncle.'

Two on the church. Two on Don Jaime's workshop. Four at the entrance to the town. Half a dozen appearing and disappearing around the Town Hall and the plaza. Tourists, if there had been any, would have whispered to each other of the iniquities of a police state, or, alternatively, have wondered from what threat of commotion a benevolent government was protecting them.

The citizens of Lazalaya were content to shrug their shoulders and speculate on the inanities which the security police must have reported to the Civil Governor. Don Baltazar, they said, ought to have stayed in his district instead of allowing his common sense to be corrupted by thirty years of law-courts and Madrid. Meanwhile the town's life continued imperturbably. In the Café Moderno the commander of the detachment of invaders occasionally joined Don Jaime and his friends at their accustomed table. In the Café Ventura turnover increased by twenty percent, since there were never less than four plainclothes security police consuming and offering liquor while they listened suspiciously to the old combatants of the Left.

'You'll drive them into revolt, Jaime,' Gil said.

'What are you talking about? They're getting more free drinks than they deserve, and have nothing to give away. The only reliable sources in Lazalaya are the Priest and the Mayor. And since they too know nothing, there's an end of it!'

'There is always Kuchler. If he tells them about the shots, they'll grill me for a week.'

'Kuchler will not be so disloyal to a friend. Besides, he considers you his agent.'

'What the hell do you mean?'

'He has organised an intelligence service. You have to

take your hat off to these Germans. The things they think of!'

'Does he pay them?'

'Yes, of course. But you're not in that class. He's got a waiter in the Moderno and another in the Ventura, two fishermen and Alonso Mejias and Enrique Jimenez.'

'What on earth can they find to tell Kuchler?' Gil exclaimed.

'What I pass on to them. They can remember it so long as they see Kuchler within a couple of hours. Double agents – that's what the cinema calls them! I have talent, and that's a fact,' the major added complacently. 'It's all in this head. The Cofradia need know nothing more, and Father Miguel only a little. On Wednesday Kuchler's partner is coming to visit the hotel site with a newspaper man from Hamburg. I shall manage them with the least possible disturbance to the authorities.'

'Jaime, it would break my uncle's heart if he were sent to Africa. He likes being Civil Governor.'

'May he enjoy it for many years! The Bishop and I have his interests always in mind.'

'I think he'd prefer to look after them himself. Why doesn't Kuchler put off his friends until Lazalaya looks less like a garrison town on a Saturday night?'

'He said they wouldn't know the difference, that they would just assume the town was well policed. Good! So they will call on me at the Town Hall at six o'clock. Nothing formal! Just to talk in private about the hotel!'

'Can I help at all?'

'Well, there's one thing I would ask of you. I have a job I promised to deliver, and I cannot arrive till nearly six. I shall leave the Vehicle in the lane behind the Café Moderno. Would you drive it back to the workshop and join me in my office afterwards? The truth is that the Vehicle is a little old-fashioned, and I would not like this newspaperman to think that the Mayor of Lazalaya cannot afford a Mercedes.'

'Of course. With pleasure.'

The request was reasonable, for few of the mayor's cronies could drive. Still, it seemed to Gil, as he strolled out of the back door of the Moderno a little after six on the Wednesday, that there was really no occasion for Kuchler's party, even if on a conducted tour of the town, to pass down the lane alongside the garbage cans, shrimp heads and vintage lavatories of the café, and no grounds for assuming – unless Kuchler mentioned it – that the Vehicle belonged to the mayor.

Lazalaya was sunk in its evening peace. The detachment of the Civil Guard had tactfully removed itself to the court-yard at the back of the Town Hall. On the balcony of the mayor's office, which overlooked the plaza, a German flag had, as a courtesy, joined the Spanish. It gave a slight air of fiesta – enough at any rate for the respectable clients of the Moderno to be a little hurt that Don Jaime had not arranged a civic reception and free drinks.

Gil entered the Vehicle, looked for the switch, remem-bered that motor-cycles did not have one and pulled an ornate little door knob of twisted wrought-iron spirals which replaced the original kick-start. The two cylinders shattered the evening with a succession of appalling backfires. Timing? A stuck valve? He cautiously opened the throttle lever. The result was a devastating explosion, as full and loud as that of a mortar, as the silencer shot off into the gutter. He tried to close the throttle. The lever had jammed. He had to use his pocket knife to loosen the holding screw. Meanwhile the machine gun, its crew having recovered from that near miss of the mortar, continued the battle.

The engine did occasionally produce a backfire or two in starting, so that Gil, sweating in the blessed silence, assumed that he hadn't known how to control it. Then at last it occurred to him why that jesuitical crook of a mayor had asked him to put away the Vehicle. Round the corner from the plaza bounced the assault car of the Civil Guard, flanked by motorcycles whose riders leaped off and took cover in the doorways, their sub-machine guns commanding the lane. Gil left the driving seat with his hands up.

Recognising both the Vehicle and its occupant, the Guards sheepishly gathered round and were joined by the customers of the Moderno, pouring out of the back door.

'I am sorry,' Gil said. 'I was trying to make it start.'

The sergeant in charge of mechanical transport examined engine and dashboard with professional interest.

'Very original,' he remarked. 'As I expected, the silencer has fallen off.'

'You'll find it down the lane somewhere.'

The sergeant recovered the silencer and easily replaced it, since it was attached to the exhaust pipe by a simple screw thread. Gil, watching, realised that Jaime must have given it a mere half turn, and he was pretty sure that it was bigger and more eaten by rust than the usual silencer. The mayor had calculated his every move in advance and, as likely as not, those of the Civil Guard as well.

The sergeant slung his sub-machine gun across his chest, entered the Vehicle and pulled the starter. The result was a booming report more menacing than any Gil himself had produced. The thread held, but the rusty end of the silencer flew screaming into the Moderno garbage cans. No one listening in the Town Hall could have any doubt that a field gun was now engaged in the local battle. Before the sergeant could close the throttle, the artillery was promptly answered by those intrepid machine gunners.

The Civil Guard stood by their motorcycles and the assault car awaiting orders. When on duty they were not supposed to laugh. They regarded the Vehicle with some embarrassment as if it had uncivically broken wind. The call to action was welcome. Far outside and to the east of the town something blew up which was certainly not a mere car engine. The detachment hurtled out of the lane, sirens shrieking, round the plaza and away into open country.

Gil hurried up the lane after them and entered the Town Hall by the side door. Running up the stairs to the mayor's office, he found Alonso Mejia and Enrique Jimenez, the two town policemen, wearing their best uniforms and white gloves, on guard in the anteroom. They saluted and opened the door of the office.

The mayor and his party were grouped around the window. Dust on Jaime's knees and on the prominence of his waistcoat suggested that he had flung himself on the

floor of the balcony at the outbreak of hostilities. The newspaperman was behind the inadequate protection of the fine
white tablecloth on which were drinks and an excellent
variety of *tapas*. Kuchler and his partner were sheltered by
the stout pillars which framed the window, and, as befitted
old combatants, still held their glasses.

Over the tumbled red roofs of the town a column of
smoke could be seen rising from the Villanueva estate,
somewhere near the far angle of the enclosure. The low sun
in the west, brilliantly lighting their dark greens on one side
of the wall and the rusty scrub on the other, made the
mist of dust and smoke in the middle look immense and
impenetrable.

Don Jaime sympathetically approached the stricken
landowner.

'On behalf of the citizens of Lazalaya I offer you my
condolences, assuring you, my dear Count, that the damage
will be made good as soon as the Government regains
control.'

This was the last straw. Jaime must be suffering from the
paranoia of power. He couldn't possibly get away with it,
however many bishops were in the background. The Vehicle
– well, that had been clever. No one could maintain that
the racket had been due to anything but a too individual
system of engineering; and, if anyone did, he would hesitate
to insist on it for fear of showing up the Civil Guard as
impulsive fools. But this outrage would call for the
immediate intervention of Madrid.

Kuchler quickly explained to his partner, who spoke no
Spanish, the identity and social significance of Gil. Both
then shook his hand with good German comradeship and
emotion. The partner remained nameless and unreal as a
figure in a nightmare. He had an obstinate, round, still face.
Beer and money had both contributed to his shape. Nothing
belonged to daily life at all except alarm at the probable
future.

'I hope that you will not allow this to affect your plans,'
Gil said, more from a vague intention of covering himself
than from cunning.

'A symbol!' Jaime broke in heartily. 'The wall around the Villanueva estate is a symbol like the police. It is of no importance!'

The Press had rejoined the party, and was making up for the interruption in the flow of hospitality. It was very properly inquisitive. The mayor willingly developed his theory of the symbols which enraged the Left. He protested that the hotel could not be included among them.

'You do not believe me?' he asked rhetorically. 'Well then, enquire of our humble citizens! Constables Jimenez and Mejias, now guarding our door in peace and with devotion, are well known to Senor Kuchler as public servants of sturdy and independent opinion whose inside knowledge of our little town is unsurpassed. We will have them in and you shall talk to them freely!'

He flung open the solid door to the anteroom and called genially for the pair. The outer door to the passage was slightly open. There was no Jimenez, no Mejias, only a splattering of blood upon the wall and an ugly gobbet on the floor. At the mayor's exclamation of horror, the four rushed into the anteroom.

'Quick! Quick!' Jaime shouted, locking the outer door. 'Here in Lazalaya we allow no scandals. All is quiet. All must always be quiet.'

He seized the tablecloth, napkins and soda syphon, and began feverishly to squirt and mop. Gil added a bottle of white wine to the pink pool. Whatever Jaime was up to, the risk was outrageous. It was urgent that the mess should vanish whether it came from the constables or, as was more likely, the pork butcher. And in any case where were they and how could they vanish for good without enquiry?

Silent and furious, he worked with Jaime, hurling the soiled linen into a cupboard. Kuchler and his partner stood by, looking very pale. The newspaper correspondent added his sandwiches and free drinks to the mess.

In three minutes from the mayor's shout of alarm no sign of the tragedy remained and the doors were open. The anteroom gave the impression that someone carrying a tray had tripped, but of what he had spilt there was no evidence.

Gil tipped down his throat the last glass which remained in his scrubbing bottle. Kuchler's partner and the journalist, though still belonging to nightmare, came back into focus. Their faces were lard-white and expressionless. They asked if they might, immediately, go down to their car. Jaime, with polite protests, accompanied them as if nothing had happened, leaving Gil and Kuchler together in his office.

'Those two poor fellows!' Kuchler cried. 'So harmless! So good-natured! Why should they be just a symbol? Revolution I can understand, but not this cold-blooded assassination. And in another month they would have retired on pension!'

'Perhaps the assailants were wounded,' Gil babbled. 'Perhaps Mejias and Jimenez have followed them . . .'

He knew very well that it didn't matter what he said, or Jaime would never have left him alone with Kuchler.

'They told me in private that they were in fear of their lives,' Kuchler said. 'I even warned Don Jaime.'

'Well, they have lasted a long time for Lazalaya,' Gil replied with some obscure intent of comfort. 'What did Jaime say?'

'He said they were devoted churchmen and always prepared to meet their end. You are – excuse me – so callous a people!'

'Sometimes we cannot find words for what we think,' Gil said, wandering helplessly off towards the bottles on the floor.

'You can find plenty for what you don't think,' Kuchler retorted with the first flash of irony Gil had ever heard from him. 'I cannot blame you or Don Jaime, but I have been grossly deceived by the Ministry of Tourism who must have known the conditions here.'

'You are going to complain to them? Wouldn't it be unwise?'

'Naturally I shall have to be very careful. I do not want to spoil my chances of selling the land to some Englishman or Dutchman who does not know the country as I do.'

It was now or never. Gil doubted the power of the Little

Brothers to keep him out of gaol, but nobody else had any interest in trying.

'Shall we cancel the whole deal?' he asked.

'You mean you would buy the site back?'

'It is my duty as a Grandee of Spain. I feel my honour is affected,' said Gil stiffly. 'All I regret is that I cannot afford to compensate you for the work on the foundations.'

'Let us leave that to our lawyers, my dear Count,' Kuchler replied, leaping at his opportunity. 'Cash or a mortgage?'

'Cash – I suppose.'

'Then you will not find me unreasonable. And now, if you will pardon me, this room . . . I am unwell. I think I shall drive straight up to Madrid.'

There was nothing to do but wait for Jaime in the safety of his office. Gil felt utterly unable to face the outside world where questions would be unanswerable and silence equally disconcerting. Meanwhile he restlessly tidied up bottles, plates and glasses so that the room looked as though some small entertainment had decorously ended.

The Civil Guard roared back into the courtyard. From the window he saw Jaime playing his part imperturbably and demanding news, like any other mayor, from an officer who was giving nothing away. Two civilian figures, formal and well-dressed, appeared from nowhere – they might have arrived in the assault car of the Civil Guard or merely been waiting behind the Town Hall – and addressed the mayor with authority. He turned into the building with one on each side.

It was too late to escape. Anyway there was no handy frontier, and nothing less would do. Jaime ushered the visitors into his office, pretending surprise and satisfaction at finding Gil there. He introduced the two civilians. A Captain Somebody. A Lieutenant Somebody. Their men in the cafés had been a joke, but these two, who had never yet been seen in the town, were disturbingly professional. They were not at all aggressive; they were smooth with the certainty of power.

It was a hundred to one that the political unrest in Laza-laya would come up before the Cabinet, but Jaime was magnificently unembarrassed. He seated himself at his desk with the two opposite, and burst into speech. He welcomed, he said, investigation at last by two such talented and distinguished officers. Ever since some absurd prank at the old nunnery had alarmed the Civil Governor – but not, he might point out, the high ecclesiastical authorities – he had hoped that Madrid would make direct enquiries.

'And let us at once get rid of the irrelevant complication of my Vehicle,' he said. 'The Conde de Villanueva will tell you what happened.'

'It wouldn't start,' said Gil feebly.

'Did you retard the spark?'

'The spark? Jaime, in this day and age you have a lever to advance or retard the spark?'

'Of course I do! She won't climb the hills without a retarded spark. For starting one must also retard it or she will backfire. Friends, I think you will agree that I cannot be held responsible because the Civil Guard panicked at a sound which all my town is accustomed to? As our glorious Generalissimo has said, local affairs should be left to the local authorities with the least possible interference by the State.'

'So this disturbance was not intended to cover up the attempt on Villanueva property?' the captain asked with a slight smile which might have been relieved or ironical.

'What attempt?'

'Ten metres of the boundary wall are blown down.'

'I will have it built up again. An accident!'

'But who did it?'

'Well, you know we don't like sending humble, decent men to prison. It's national policy.'

'Not so much of national policy if you please, Don Jaime! We are as aware of it as you are.'

'Patience, captain! I was on the point of explaining. The contractors who are building our hotel naturally have a store of explosives. Well, and we have a small community of fishermen. One should never be next to the other. To cut a long story short, they stole some explosives for use at sea. This was reported to me and I took the action which the father of a family should take. "Friends," I said, for I am accustomed to being obeyed, "who did this I do not know and I do not want to know. If the whole lot is destroyed at once, I will forget it."

'Well, it appears that they let it off close to the Villanueva wall, which was upwind, so that the hillside should not catch fire. That was sensible. A morning's work will repair the damage. But they chose for their explosion a moment when I was entertaining distinguished foreigners. As a result, our hotel, the valued, indispensable project which will give life to our town is in danger.'

'You accept this story?' the Captain asked Gil.

'Of course. I have no enemies.'

'He has been congratulated by the Syndicate of Agricultural Workers,' added the mayor proudly.

'And you are prepared to swear that there is no political unrest in Lazalaya?'

'None. I am sure that all the reports of your agents will agree.'

The lieutenant, entering the conversation for the first time, remarked sourly that it was the only point on which they did agree. The captain, raising his eyebrows in astonishment that the reports of secret agents should be mentioned at all, gathered up his subordinate and left.

'Thank God it wasn't about Jimenez and Mejias!' Gil exclaimed.

'Don't worry! You see I have talent. Father Miguel will write to the Civil Governor about their pensions, and after him the Bishop.'

'Damn their pensions! What's happened to them?'

'Nothing! Nothing!' the mayor answered soothingly. 'But administratively speaking it presents a problem. Did you notice the slaughterman's van at the side door when you arrived?'

'I don't know. There was something.'

'Well, that's how they left. He'll return their uniforms this evening. Lazalaya cannot afford new ones.'

'Suppose he talks?'

'Then he won't get the contract for the hotel.'

'There isn't going to be a hotel, Jaime.'

'And how is he to know that? Sometimes I think you left your intelligence in America.'

'But it must all come out! Tomorrow at the latest!'

'Then let it! Look! What has always been the defence of the humble? To make the authorities look fools, but in such a way that they cannot resent it. Gil, the town is proud of you.'

'The police won't be.'

'This is too serious for the police. The Civil Governor is bound to investigate the affair in person. Besides, he's in it up to the neck.'

'I tell you, Jaime, he'll sit with his fingertips together and sacrifice the pair of us.'

'Not if he can score one up for himself. Let's go over to the Moderno! It is time to calm the spirits of our fellow citizens.'

They certainly needed it. Lazalaya was buzzing with rumour, and the mayor's café table was immediately surrounded, as if it had been a roulette table, by those who were privileged to sit there and others who had at least the right to lean over their shoulders.

When the crowd had thinned down to a dozen intimate friends, Jaime told his story of the damage to the Villanueva wall. The tale instantly became fact. No doubt, with a slight change of emphasis, it was. Gil, listening with such admiration as he could manage and once again privileged to pay for drinks, considered that a few explosives had indeed been stolen and that Jaime, as his price for keeping quiet, blackmailed the culprits into setting them off against the wall.

At about eleven the disappearance of Jimenez and Mejias was reported to the newsroom. They had not returned to barracks and had apparently vanished into the air. Jaime, who had just received a gigantic omelette from the Moderno's kitchen, refused to be impressed. All he could say was that the missing constables had been on duty at the Town Hall when he went out to say goodbye to Kuchler's partner and that they had not been there when he returned.

He only hoped that no accident had happened, such as might be feared when an innocent town was under the threat of fire-arms in excitable hands.

Next morning, after one look at Lazalaya, Gil decided to remain at home. The women and the police had taken over. From every balcony and doorstep the high-pitched whispers criss-crossed the alleys with stories of confirmed murder and expected rape. The Civil Guard and mysterious strangers were sternly occupied and had at last a definite case for their notebooks. Jaime, in the intervals of replacing the old silencer on his Vehicle, was hounding on the search for Jimenez and Mejias and accompanying the police to improbable remoteness where, alive or dead, they might be found. There was no fish, because the fishermen had decided to remain at sea.

After three days it was at last with a feeling of relief that Gil received the writ of the Civil Governor. He packed a bag with such necessities as would, he thought, be permitted to a prisoner awaiting trial. Jaime, who was also in the police car and dressed in the black suit of thick cloth which he used for funerals and official visits, carried nothing but a packet of ham sandwiches presented, with a blessing, by Father Miguel.

They were escorted to the secretary's room, in which, sitting bolt upright against the wall, were two very obvious bodyguards. The personage closeted with Don Baltasar was plainly of Cabinet rank. He had a powerful, military voice which rumbled through the double doors. The high, legal tones of the Civil Governor sounded in contrast like the yapping of some small, conscientious dog.

There was at last a moment of comparative silence. The telephone in the secretary's room demanded their immediate presence. As soon as they entered the great office, the row broke out again. Gil recognised the Caesarian bald head and sturdy figure of the Director of Internal Security, responsible only to the Chief of State.

'. . . and the Press! For the sake of the Ministry of Tourism we have been compelled to censor the despatch of a respected German correspondent. And all this because of incapacity on the part of the Civil Governor who is utterly unable to explain the cause of the unrest!'

'I am bound to depend on my police and yours, General, for information,' Don Baltasar retorted. 'I have no more and no less than you. By the way, allow me to present the Conde de Villanueva and Don Jaime Caruncho, Mayor of Lazalaya.'

'Delighted! . . . It is an intolerable position. Where are we? With the Mafia in Sicily? Either no one knows anything or everybody is afraid to talk. You there! You are the mayor. These Germans tell us you badly wanted this hotel. Well, you aren't going to get it. And I am much inclined to send in a battalion of troops to assist you in your administration.'

'We shall do our best to be hospitable, my General, though the resources of our town are small,' replied Jaime with formal courtesy.

'And you, Villanueva! Are you going to maintain in front of me all these lies about your wall?'

Whether or not Gil had told any lies – he thought that on the whole he had not, though God alone knew how many he had condoned – this was deliberately impolite and not to be borne from any upstart of a government employee, however exalted. He drew his steel at once.

'I had considered,' he replied, 'that it was only these absurd foreigners and the Civil Guard who made a habit of seeing revolutionaries under their beds. It is a shock to me that I must also include persons whom I, my fellow citizens and our beloved Leader are accustomed to trust.'

'Your honour is as precious to me as my own,' the general answered with ironical formality. 'I shall therefore appeal to it. You were present on the occasion when, according to the Ministry of Tourism, these Germans saw the floor and walls of the mayor's anteroom spattered with blood. Is it so or not?'

'On my honour I saw no human blood whatever. But perhaps – it is only my suggestion – red wine had flowed too freely.'

'May I enquire what this new accusation is?' asked Don Baltasar.

'Two municipal police of Lazalaya have been murdered.'

'I regret that I know nothing.'

'It seems one could murder half the province without your Excellency's knowledge.'

'That of course is so, if I am not given a copy of the report. The source of your information?'

'My sources are the German Embassy and the Ministry of Tourism. The Mayor of Lazalaya here will confirm that an investigation is proceeding.'

'The mayors of small towns are not always in touch with the wider world, General. Can you give me the names of these two victims?'

'Alonso Mejias and Enrique Jimenez.'

'Ah, indeed they are familiar,' said the Civil Governor. 'A question of pensions. It may be necessary, I fear, to appeal to the Cabinet. The unflagging interest of the Chief of State in the spiritual welfare of the people, which of course you and I fully share . . .'

Don Baltasar rang for his secretary.

'The Mejias–Jimenez file, please.'

'Then you do know something?'

'I had no knowledge that they were dead, General. Now, let me see! Ah, yes,' he went on, leafing through a file which seemed to Gil to have acquired a surprising number of documents in a short time. 'These two policemen heard the irresistible call of religion a month before they were due to retire. It is regrettable that they should have deserted their post without orders. It complicates so abominably their pension rights.'

'They aren't murdered?'

'There is no mention of it in the file. It's the pension which has been referred to . . .'

'Then where the devil are they?'

The Civil Governor lowered his eyes in mild disapproval of this military and overbearing language.

'My dear General, upon a sudden impulse – who are we to question it? – these two simple devotees, perhaps

176

encouraged by their parish priest, perhaps alarmed by the recent disturbance of their long and meditative peace in municipal service, have taken their provisional vows and entered the Convent of the Little Brothers of St Macario.'

Chaplain to the Embassy

Padre Francisco was listening. The arc of the mountains encircled him on all sides but one, where shone the deserted sea. There was a fast, clear stream at his feet, and on the further bank a meadow, very green and studded with white boulders and jewelled with low flowers in the short grass. It was spring, and there were children in the meadow; one of them held a lamb by the forefeet and played that he was teaching it to dance. Men said there was a war in Spain, but Spain was beyond Galicia and Galicia beyond the mountains. No railway crossed the mountains, nor any way but one, and that unkindly to horse and man. Caladonga had its cove by the sea, but only the fishermen of the village ever landed there, for it offered no open entry to the passing craft.

Padre Francisco was listening to music: the music of a pipe which trilled and warbled from a bank of yellow iris by the stream. The child did not hear it, though his feet moved in time to the measure. The lamb heard, and its head was turned towards the stream. Padre Francisco heard. His cloth did not protect him from the pipe of Pan, for he was innocent and beloved. He raised his hand and blessed the pipe and its player. All creatures in Caladonga, seen or unseen, were his flock.

There was no shame, either of men or of the Others, among his flock, for he did not accuse. He knew the spring upon the hillside, visited at the new moon by the unmarried girls. He left untouched the grains of wheat scattered upon the high stone which stood in a ring of uncut grass. He was silent when the returning fishermen poured wine into the sea opposite a silver-sanded cave. Padre Francisco had blessed these sanctuaries. He said:

178

'If there is need of your charity, give, my children. But give in the name of the Most High and pray for him that receives.'

For sixty years he had tended his parish – a white, red-roofed village and its little plain, forgotten of all save the carrier and his mule. He had never left it, nor had he ever tired of it. His eyes were thankful and rejoiced in the detail of the earth as if he had been reborn each morning with the sun. His faith was humble and complete. His theology was the theology of Caladonga. He read the pastorals of a bishop whom he had never seen, bidding him guard against this and that heresy, and this and that deadly sin. 'Nay, but there is no deadly sin,' said Padre Francisco. Caladonga had no sin that he could not readily forgive, and to him Caladonga was the world.

As he sat on the bank of the steam, a peasant came to him and saluted him. His name was Castor-He-of-the-Oranges. He had no other surname. Castor stood as if ashamed, with bent head and folded hands, waiting for the old man to speak to him. Padre Francisco looked at him sorrowfully.

'Does it trouble you still, Castor?' he asked.

'Yes. You must exorcise it, padre. It will not go away.'

'Castor, Castor, that which has been created should not be hurt.'

'Then do it gently, padre! My house is unhappy, and you must help us. We cannot sleep for the noises and the drifting lights, but because you told us to be forgiving we have borne with them. We summoned the *curandera*, the wise woman . . .'

'That was sin, my son,' interrupted Padre Francisco, shaking his silver head.

'I know it, padre – but what were we to do? The spirit pinched her and she ran away shrieking. That too we could forgive, for the *curandera* was insolent and demanded money. But now we dare not be patient any longer. This morning I found my two oxen tied together by the hairs of their tails. They were sweating with panic, and must be bled

179

or they will die. Without our oxen we should starve. You must help us, padre.'

'So be it then,' said Padre Francisco.

He rose. The eddies of the breeze played around his cassock, moulding it to his spare figure with love, as if he had been a young girl in whom the winds delighted.

Together they walked along the stream. When they came to the village bridge Padre Francisco stopped.

'Castor,' he asked, 'if it were a mischievous boy who played these tricks on you, you would not cast him out of your house for ever?'

'But it is not a boy,' said the peasant simply.

The old man sighed, and went on alone towards his church.

Castor with his wife and children waited for him at the door of their white cottage. The faded blue of the lintels and twisted balconies held all the colours of the sky. Two orange trees stood in the garden with late fruit still showing like flowers among the leaves. The spirit haunted the house because he loved it, not because he must.

Now wearing his stole and carrying a flask of holy water, Francisco came to them and blessed them. Humbly he prayed that he might be worthy, and forthwith began the conjuration. Severe and terrible was the Latin, but Padre Francisco's voice was gentle.

'I adjure thee, Old Serpent –' he began.

But it was no command. He was the superior and knew that he would be obeyed; therefore he had no need of vehemence.

'*Audi ergo, Satana, et time*! Hear therefore, Satan, and fear! Conquered and prostrate, retire!'

Padre Francisco meant what he said, for it was a naughty deed to tie his parishioner's oxen together by the tails. He hoped that the spirit would not be very frightened, but he intended that it should retire.

Five psalms he said, and sprinkled the house with holy water; then again five psalms and for a third time five. The last was 'Ecce quam bonum' – behold how good and how pleasant it is for brethren to dwell together in unity! As the old man intoned the psalm, he heard the words echoed to a melody that soared in a golden treble over his voice.

'*Dominus vobiscum*,' said Padre Francisco.

'*Et cum spiritu tuo*,' answered They-of-the-Oranges.

'*Et cum spiritu tuo*,' said a grateful voice as of one passing through the doorway.

Padre Francisco walked back to the church and took off his stole. Then he went down to the seashore and sat upon the sand of the cove, for he was sorrowful and wished to be alone.

The cove was like an inland pool. The sea entered through an archway, and above the packed swell of the Atlantic the sheep pastured on a roof of green turf. From the horns of the crescent-shaped beach where Padre Francisco sat, two low cliffs converged upon the archway; through the entry he could see an anchored boat lifting and falling on the open sea, and beyond it the horizon. At his feet the water was pale green, transparent over the shelving sand; under the cliffs to right and to left of him it was blue and purple, and brown shadows glided about their business.

There indeed was Padre Francisco in the midst of love. The shepherd above the arch called to him good-day. The fisherman in the boat waved a hand, and held up a creel of rock bass for him to see. A cormorant which sat like an old serpent – it was Padre Francisco's metaphor – upon a ledge of rock straightened its sinuous neck, swooped and landed in the ripples at his feet. The great black bird sidled up to him, blinking its eyes. It looked at him long and fearlessly, as if judging his worth. Its pupils were red and inset with curious reflections.

'What is good and what is evil?' thought Padre Francisco. 'I can see no evil, and therefore I will pray for guidance.'

Now this was not accounted a sin to Padre Francisco, for, as the whims of a sick child may command its parents, so were Heaven and Hell disturbed by the vagaries of this earth. 'What is good?' asked the advance guard of the angels. 'What is evil?' asked the left wing of the armies of Satan.

And Satan went to and fro upon the earth and longed for

the ancient days, for he could not recognise his servants or his enemies. There were those who destroyed the Church for the sake of Faith, and those who destroyed Faith for the sake of the Church. Nor did death decide the loyalties of a perverse generation. Austere, religious souls floated to Heaven and declared themselves atheists. The worldly plunged downwards into Hell, where they were found to be clerics of blameless life and irreproachable morality.

But Satan knew that the earth, though it was but a little earth, was greatly beloved in Heaven as in Hell. Therefore he drew up a great document in Hebrew and Latin and letters of fire, which began 'FORASMUCH AS WE SATAN ARE AT A LOSS' and resolved itself into magnificent periods upon the inalienable rights of the High Contracting Parties. But in Heaven his meaning was understood. It was made known to him that he had only to choose an acceptable ambassador for Heaven to be represented at his Court.

He asked for Michael, since they had been friends in the fresh morning of eternity, and as enemies they had respected one another. And Michael took up his residence in Hell, heralded by four secretaries to the Embassy who were the four beasts full of eyes before and behind.

Many were the banquets and rejoicings at the Embassy. The windless night of the damned was rich with music. David came down and played the harp for them, and Nero's violin wailed upwards into chaos borne on the winged feet of Saint Cecilia at the organ. Pan composed a symphony on dawn, and played it on his pipe, accompanied by the trumpeters of an Archangel's Guard.

And on a certain evening Satan and Michael walked in the garden of the Embassy and wept together that the simplicity of earth was lost.

'There are many who believe in you,' said the Devil, 'but so few left who believe in us. And now the time has come for one of the last of them to die. May we give him a gift, Michael?'

'Why not?' asked Michael.

'Because he is one of your servants,' Satan explained. 'A certain Padre Francisco of Caladonga in Galicia.'

'I am weary of Spanish priests,' said Michael.

'I am weary of Spanish anarchists,' retorted Satan.

'What has he done for your people?' asked Michael.

'He has pitied them,' said the Devil. 'By all I hear, I think he is a saint.'

'And a Christian too?' the Archangel asked.

'As in the ancient days, Michael, when saints were saints and the Temptor tempted.'

And Michael perceived that, exchanging one courtesy for another, he could obtain for his Embassy the one dignity that it lacked.

'Satan,' he said, 'I need a chaplain.'

'I am old,' answered the Devil, 'but not a bigot. Myself, I would willingly attend a service. But I do not know if my people would stand it. I really do not.'

'Even if my Chaplain were Padre Francisco of Caladonga?'

'I will have a look at him,' said Satan.

Now it was at this moment in the time of earth that the cormorant sidled up to Padre Francisco.

'You can have your chaplain,' said the Devil, restoring his spirit to eternity. 'But what of the gift my people would present to him?'

'We give you his death,' answered Michael.

Padre Francisco lay back upon the sand with his hands crossed at his throat. He was tired, and it was good to feel the strength of his beloved earth against his back and the warmth of the sun upon his body. He closed his eyes. A ripple of water like the streaming arrow at the bows of a light boat formed in the archway and curled towards him across the cove. In the brown and purple shadows of the cliffs seven ripples formed upon his right hand, and seven ripples upon his left. Smaller than the first they were, and shaped like cupid's bows; they might have been moulded to the breasts of women advancing through the water; they took on the colours of the sun like little breaking waves. The sheep above the arch moved away, and the shepherd

183

followed them; there was, as it were, a sea haze forming upon the turf, and he was afraid to stay. Behind Padre Francisco the grasses of the fields waved in the wind, but there were many winds from many quarters, and the ranks of the flowers bent and straightened as the spirits of earth passed on towards the cove.

The ripple that had formed under the arch reached the shore, and Padre Francisco was awakened by the singing of many voices. He sat up, and then leapt to his feet in wonder and in joy at those who compassed him about. His lips parted and his eyes were full of tears. He opened his arms as if to gather into them the massed armies of the spirits, and he cried:

'Lo! Before I die I have seen the glory of the living earth!'

The angels caught up Padre Francisco from the midst of his lovers, and took him into Heaven and robed and anointed him. The Saints received him into their number and led him out to the gates, chanting in procession. Then, olive-crowned, borne upon the wings of doves with satyrs dancing before and behind, guarded by the drawn swords of the squadrons of the Prince of Darkness, Padre Francisco entered into Hell.